OHIO
DOMINICAN
UNIVERSITY™

SINCE 1911

Donated by
Floyd Dickman

Strong at the Heart

How It Feels to Heal from Sexual Abuse

Strong at the Heart

How It Feels to Heal from Sexual Abuse

Carolyn Lehman

Melanie Kroupa Books
Farrar, Straus and Giroux
New York

Distributed in Canada by Douglas & McIntyre Publishing Group
Printed in the United States of America
Designed by Jay Colvin
First edition, 2005
1   3   5   7   9   10   8   6   4   2

www.fsgkidsbooks.com

Library of Congress Cataloging-in-Publication Data
Strong at the heart : how it feels to heal from sexual abuse / [compiled] by Carolyn Lehman.
      p.   cm.
    ISBN-13: 978-0-374-37282-8
    ISBN-10: 0-374-37282-9
    1. Sexual abuse victims—United States—Case studies—Juvenile literature.
    2. Child sexual abuse—United States—Case studies—Juvenile literature.
    I. Lehman, Carolyn.

    HV6592.S87 2005
    362.76'4—dc22

                                                        2004056280

Photographs on pages 38 and 46 courtesy of Kelly St. John, on page 94 courtesy of Tino
Plank, and on pages 106 and 109 courtesy of Akaya Windwood. All other photographs by
Carolyn Lehman.

For Peter, Carmela and Kit
who walk with me

and Jacob, Ben,
Kristen and Louise
who run on ahead

Contents

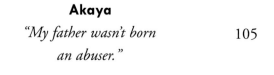

Foreword

I have had the honor of working with survivors of sexual abuse for the past twenty years. Although most of my work has been with adults, I know firsthand the challenges young survivors face. When I was a girl, my grandfather came into my room one night to tell me a story, reached under the covers, and started to touch me. From that moment on, my life was never the same.

I wish I'd had a book like *Strong at the Heart* to show me that I was not alone, that someday I would figure out how to heal the hurt, learn to trust, and go on to create the rich and satisfying life that I have today. If I'd had a resource like the one you now hold in your hands, I wouldn't have had to suffer in silence for so long.

This powerful book is filled with the distinct, diverse voices of people who experienced rape, molestation, and incest when they were young. With remarkable honesty they tell how they stopped feeling victimized and reclaimed their lives. They describe the choices they made, the people they turned to, and the inner strength they discovered.

The personal stories in *Strong at the Heart* will move you, inform you, and inspire you. They will show you what is possible in your own life, in the lives of people you care about, and in the world.

Look into the faces of these strong survivors. Listen to their voices. Let them be the signposts for your own healing journey.

Wishing you courage and peace,

Laura Davis,

author of *The Courage to Heal* and

I Thought We'd Never Speak Again

Introduction

The world breaks everyone and afterward many
are strong at the broken places.
—Ernest Hemingway, *A Farewell to Arms*

NO ONE KNOWS FOR SURE HOW MANY SURVIVORS of childhood sexual abuse there are, because sexual abuse is one of North America's most underreported crimes. The most frequently cited estimates are that about one out of every three girls and one in six boys are sexually abused in some way before they turn eighteen. Half of all rape victims are children. No matter how you look at the statistics, there are a lot of survivors. In this book you will meet us, face-to-face.

If you have experienced sexual abuse or assault, this book is for you. You will find out how other teens and adults are healing from abuse and what might work for you, too.

If you have not been abused, this book may give you insight into the survivors in your own life. You will see the important roles that friends and family members have in these stories. You may get ideas about what you can do to make the world safer for kids.

Most teens and children who are sexually violated experience abuse in isolation. They cope the best they can. In these interviews, you'll see a variety of ways kids try to deal with sexual abuse and the often overwhelming emotions that come with it.

Before healing can start, the abuse has to stop. Some of the survivors in this book fought back or made other choices that ended the abuse. Sooner or later they broke out of isolation. They all told someone—a sister, a friend, a police officer, a counselor.

As you'll see in these interviews, what happens next is not a one-size-fits-all process. People are different. They are hurt in different ways and they heal differently, too.

Still, the resilient survivors in this book have these things in common:

- They spoke up—again and again if they had to—and got help.
- They listened to their own feelings and decided what worked for them and what didn't.
- Over time, they connected with other people—family members, therapists, other survivors, friends—and received emotional support and practical help.
- They gave healing the time and attention it deserves.
- They took action and made choices that made their lives better.
- They never gave up on themselves.

Almost everyone found creative ways to express their feelings—writing, filmmaking, creating music, and playing sports. Many people relied on spiritual support, even those who didn't consider themselves religious. They all needed someone to encourage them and guide them, but when it came to healing, as seventeen-year-old Jonathan said, "It's an inside job."

Healing doesn't mean living as if the abuse never happened. No one can undo the past. But by making conscious decisions, these people put their lives back together in ways that made sense to them, that led to the future *they* chose for themselves.

Although every person's story is unique, for this book I sought out interviews that—in general—reflect the demographics of sexual abuse in North America. My search took me from California to New England, from the New Jersey Pine Barrens to a Native reservation in Canada.

Sexual abuse happens in every social, racial, geographic, cultural, and economic group. According to Department of Justice statistics, more than 90 percent of sexual offenders are known and trusted by their victims; about half of offenders are family members. Most are men, some are women. Teens and children abuse other kids, too.

I've included interviews with adults in this book because healing takes place over time. Kelly coped well with abduction and rape when she was a teen, but in college she needed to look at that experience again—and she turned it into an Emmy-award-winning film. Some of the ways kids cope can be destructive. Arturo got involved in drugs to cover his feelings of shame. He was twenty-one when he made the choice to get off drugs and deal with the underlying hurt. Some people take much longer. The adults' stories may help you look ahead to the rewards of healing or give you insight into the adult survivors in your own life.

Healing from abuse doesn't just mean the healing of individuals. When children are hurt, our whole society suffers. Many people are working to make our communities safer for kids and more supportive of people trying to overcome abuse. The last chapter focuses on three nineteen-year-old college students who are bringing healing to their campus community.

Whatever your experience, learning about abuse can be stressful. It's normal to be disturbed by the idea of someone hurting a child. If reading these stories brings up emotions that you don't expect or reminds you of painful events in your own life, take a break, talk with a parent or friend. Or you can call one of the 24-hour hotlines listed on page 135. They are confidential and free.

Like the survivors in this book, I was sexually abused in childhood. An important part of my own healing was meeting others who had had similar experiences. For me, nothing else was as powerful as looking into the faces of people who had gone through what I was struggling with, knowing that they'd made it, and hearing how. That inspired me to create this book so that you, too, could learn about healing from the real experts—other survivors, regular people like yourself. As sixteen-year-old Sheena said, "This book is like a healing circle that anyone can join."

The people you are about to meet are heroes in the truest sense of the word. As kids they survived danger, violence, and betrayal. In healing, they discovered truths about themselves, helped others on the way, and enlarged their capacity for love and for joy.

They chose to tell their personal stories and be photographed for this book so that you could see the true face of healing. In different words and different accents, each of them said to me, "Tell other kids they are not alone. Tell them to hang in there. Tell them they can get through this and have good lives."

Sexual abuse is heartbreaking. It can cut to the very core of who we are and who we will become. But you and those you know can heal. Like the survivors in this book, you can become strong at the heart.

Strong at the Heart

How It Feels to Heal from Sexual Abuse

Jenner

WHAT HAPPENED WAS THIS: the summer before tenth grade my girlfriends and I went to a party. I guess the parents were away for the
weekend. Anyhow, there were no adults around. There was this big
bottle of tequila and I was taking shots. I was fourteen, it was my first
experience with alcohol, and I overdid it. I asked my girlfriends to
take care of me because I was really out of it. Most of the night they
sat next to me outside on the deck, talking.

This guy I'd once gone to school with sat down with us. He and
one of my friends decided that the three of us were going to go to the
store. I was like, "Sure." I was so naïve and trusting, it never crossed
my mind that something bad could happen.

the ride

I don't even know if we ever got to the store. It ended up that he drove
us back to the party and dropped off my girlfriend. He said that we
were going to go to his other friend's house to say hi and that we'd
come right back.

So I ended up with just him. He drove somewhere, I don't know where. I was blacked out, totally out of it. I woke up to him having sex with me.

I was a virgin and in shock. I was so drunk I couldn't do anything to stop him. I didn't want to be there. I didn't even like this guy.

I felt so separated from what was happening, like my body was in one place and the rest of me in another. It was as if my mind was saying, "This isn't really happening. This couldn't be happening to me."

Afterward, he dropped me off at the party and I stumbled out of the car. The party was breaking up, so I went home with one of my girlfriends and spent the night at her house.

The next morning, when I woke up, I was really confused. My friends had said they'd take care of me and they hadn't. I felt so uncomfortable about my body. I was worried because I didn't think he'd used a condom. And when I tried to talk with my friend about it all, her reaction was like, "Hey, it's no big deal. What do you expect? This kind of thing happens at parties." That's when I felt the most alone.

For a long time I thought that if I told people what happened to me, even my parents, they would think I was a bad person and blame me for it. I even blamed myself.

I blamed myself because I'd been drinking. Somehow I felt that made what he did my fault. And I kept thinking, "What was I wearing? Was it something provocative?" Now I realize that it didn't matter *what* I was wearing. How can anyone ever think they can force themselves on you like that? It's so far from being okay.

My parents had moved, so that fall I started at a new high school. A year later, I told a friend there about what happened and she said, "You were raped." It took someone else saying it out loud for me to acknowledge that that's what happened.

When this thing happened to me, I didn't know how to handle it. At some level I guess I was angry about it, but I couldn't say it out loud or even admit it to myself. You know, when girls get mad or start a fight, they're told, "Be a good girl. Just behave." Girls are expected to be cheery and nice and not confront people. We aren't given tools to deal with anger.

In my senior year I did a really stupid thing. Through friends from my old school I heard that the guy who did this had been telling people what he did, saying things like, "Yeah, I think she was a virgin!" as if that made him more of a man or something.

I was embarrassed, but my friends were angry for me. In revenge, they decided to blow up his parents' mailbox, and I went along with it. Word got out and we got caught.

I was so scared. I spent the whole day in my room, pacing and crying, expecting a phone call from the police, trying to figure out how I was going to tell my parents—not just about the vandalism but also about the event that triggered it. That was one of the hardest things I've ever had to do: tell my parents.

For more than two years I'd kept the rape a secret from my parents. When I finally told them, it seemed like they were more angry at me for scaring his family than at him for what he had done to me. Now I understand that they didn't know what to say. The whole thing must have been so hard for my mom and dad to hear. Later on we were able to talk about the sexual assault part and my parents were supportive—but at first it felt like they cared more about these other people than about me.

I was put on probation for the vandalism. Part of probation was that I had to go to counseling. It wasn't something I chose or wanted to do, but it helped to talk, especially about some of my friends' and my parents' reactions. My mom came one time and that was good.

Then I decided to report the rape. My mom went with me to the police station. I went up to the counter, in this room full of strangers, and said, "I want to report a rape."

A male officer took me into a tiny, bare room, like a holding cell with cold cement walls. He shut the door. It was just me and him in there. He kept pressuring me with questions I couldn't answer, things like, "What color were his eyes?" and when I didn't know the answers, he asked me to guess. I felt like he didn't believe what I was saying. He called what happened date rape and I didn't like that. We definitely were not dating!

Nothing came of the report, although the officer said he would talk to the guy. But I think it was helpful for me to make that stand, to say, "Hey, what happened isn't okay," and then do something about it.

Emotionally, I still felt numb. My counselor tried to get me to break out of my shell. She kept encouraging me to get at my own anger by cussing, yelling, and hitting a pillow, things like that. But it just wasn't there. All these other people had clearly defined emotions about what happened to me. But I didn't. I felt like an observer of my life.

I think I was afraid of my feelings. I'd never had to deal with anger before—not anger that deep, not rage—and I didn't know how it would come out. I thought it would scare people. It scared me.

So my brain tried to deal with the rape by rationalizing it away, saying, "It's over. Just forget it." But something else inside me kept bringing me back to it, saying, "There are important things to be dealt with here." It took years, but my brain finally shut up and my emotions broke through.

breaking through

On my college campus there was a candlelight vigil for a woman who'd been gang-raped in town. She'd gone to a party and had a lot to drink, and when she went outside to look for her friend, these guys jumped her.

My friends and I went to the rally to show support for her. There was a long line of people waiting for their turn at the microphone. Each person spoke to her and some also talked about their own experiences with sexual violence. Then she got up to speak and suddenly it hit me hard.

I was flooded with emotion for her. I was so angry. And not just angry for her. Angry for all the people who had been hurt this way. Angry that it happened to me.

It's hard to put into words, but it was such a relief to *feel*. I wanted to cry and scream and hit and hug people all at the same time. This is what the counselor and my parents and my friends had felt! I'd been so numb emotionally. Suddenly the block between me and my emotions was gone. It wasn't just that I could feel again, but I could see how it all fit together, too, like when you lift the hood of a car and see how the insides work.

Sitting next to me was this guy I was dating at the time. He didn't know what was going on with me, but he saw that I was upset and he put his arm around me. It felt so good to be supported by this man, to realize that he cared about me, and that I didn't feel angry at all men because of what one guy did.

my song

After the vigil I was so full of emotions. My friends were sitting around the living room in our dorm suite talking, but I couldn't sit still. This volcano was erupting inside of me. I knew something really big was happening and I couldn't push it away, it was coming up so fast.

I needed to be by myself so I could figure out what was going on. I went to my room, locked the door, and started writing.

Words and feelings poured out of me. I was writing so fast I couldn't stop my hand. I wrote cuss words. I wrote what I felt. I wrote about what happened to me. I wrote without self-censoring and without the intention of editing it later. What I found out was that it's easier for me to know what I feel when it's just me and my pen and paper or my guitar than when there's someone like a counselor trying to pull it out of me.

Over the next several days, the pages of words turned into lyrics. I'd already been working on this three-chord melody the week before, so I started using it with some of the words. I liked how they came together; the song was raw and to the point. For about a week, this one song was the only thing I could do. I worked on it for hours every day, then I'd go walking in the woods and come back and work on it some more. In class, the music and lyrics kept playing in my mind. New thoughts would emerge and I'd rush back to my dorm to try them out.

Writing that song was my catharsis. It gave me a way to step into the experience, really feel it for the first time. It was such a relief to go ahead and feel the anger and express it in a way that was constructive. Maybe that's what healing is: allowing your emotions to run their course.

Once I finally got to my feelings, they began to sort themselves out. I became more forgiving of myself, more understanding of how my friends and my parents reacted. I saw that I had a lot more choices about my life. I had to trust myself to go through the anger and all the other emotions so that I could get to a better, stronger place.

Then I was asked to sing my song at a Take Back the Night rally. That was a thrilling experience. It isn't a song I'd share with just any

audience. It's pretty raw and there's a lot of cuss words in it. But people there were ready to hear it. And afterward they came up to me—guys, even—and told me how much they appreciated it.

Then, just recently, I was giving a concert at a coffeehouse with my accompanist, John. The mood was right. We decided to do it. And the audience response was great.

virginity

There's a line in the song, "So go on and tell your friends of a girl you stole." He did steal that—my girlhood and my first sexual experience.

When he talked about it at school, I was so humiliated. The words in the song give the shame back to him. Okay, go tell people! When he talks about it, he's admitting to doing this really horrible thing. Maybe someone who hears him will react in a way that makes him realize what he did was wrong.

What happened was sex, but it wasn't making love. He messed with my body in a sexual way, but he can't touch the inside, the me, the soul—the part of me that loves people.

I lost my virginity to a person I didn't even like. But since then, I've found out that I am capable of really loving a man and expressing it sexually. I own my sexuality. I'm glad I have that. It's something only I can give.

changes

It happened so long ago, but it's something I'll never forget. And it's okay not to forget. Forgetting would just make me more vulnerable again.

I've become less of an optimist. I no longer believe that everybody is good and the world will look out for me. Now I understand that it's up to me to take care of myself. I still go out and dance and even drink some with friends. But I watch my intake. I'm careful about who I'm with and how I'll get home.

And when I look at a man, I don't just see a man. I am aware that he could be a potential rapist. I really want to know him before being alone with him.

Now I believe that whatever I feel is okay to feel—even if it isn't nice or convenient or acceptable—because that's what's coming out of me and it's real. It's a powerful thing, actually, to embrace all of your feelings—to not run from anger or pretend it isn't alive inside you, but to face it, cultivate it, turn it into a strength.

All of our feelings are important. Without emotions, who are we?

Jonathan

WHEN I WAS THIRTEEN YEARS OLD, snorting coke, suicidal as hell, feeling like I had not a friend in the world, if you would have told me "Life gets better. You are here for a purpose, you're gonna help people," I would have told you to go to hell. I'm sorry, excuse my language. I would have said, "You're outta your freakin' mind."

If I'd never talked to anybody about what Father Jim did to me, if I'd never gotten help, the only way I would have been known today is by a headstone. Or maybe my friends would be visiting me in jail.

But now I'm seventeen years old, and I'm known all over the state for my public speaking and for helping other kids.

church and family

I grew up in a very strict Catholic family. I'm one of twelve kids, the sixth child down. I have six brothers and five sisters and there's another brother who's adopted. Ten nieces and nephews and two more on the way. My older brothers are all plumbers and tattoo-covered animals. We're just an original bunch of rowdy boys.

Anything that had to do with the church, my family was involved. Until I was in fifth grade, all of us kids went to Catholic school. Me and my brothers were all altar servers. My mom taught religion classes. Both my parents were eucharistic ministers. One year my parents got the Medal of Meritorious Honor from the bishop. We were just totally devoted to the church. The church was our life.

My parents were always there for us no matter what, but with so many kids it was hard financially. The church helped us out a lot. Sometimes they'd bring food over for us. One Christmas they gave presents to my parents to give to me and my brothers and sisters.

A lot of priests were family friends. It wasn't anything out of the ordinary to see a priest just pop in the door to spend time with us or stop over for dinner.

My dad was a police officer for twenty-eight years, always working long shifts, five to seven days a week. When he wasn't working he was sleeping. He had it rough. My mom was just constantly on her feet taking care of us, running us somewhere, cleaning the house, getting stuff done for school.

Thursday was the day my mom got to go out. She'd go shopping and we'd order pizza. Father Jim would come over and babysit us, to help her out a little. He'd give us our baths and put us to bed.

someone special

When Father Jim came over, I always ran right up to him. My father was my hero, but he worked such long hours I didn't get to see him much. Father Jim was a male figure for me to look up to and I seemed to be his favorite.

In a big family, you don't get a lot of attention. Father Jim gave me his full, devoted attention. He told me he loved me. And I loved having somebody to look up to, somebody who loved me, just me, not the rest of my brothers and sisters. I was proud of the attention.

Now that I look back on it, I'm just starting to realize what was going on then. He did simple things, like he would pull my waistband out and look down my pants. He'd say, "Oh, cool underwear." Maybe I had on Spiderman underwear or something. I was a little kid, eight years old.

I used to sit on his lap when we were watching TV. He would do things like place his hands over my privates. I'm thinking now that maybe that was to test me to see if I was going to say anything. At the time, I didn't think anything about it. A priest was God on earth to me. He couldn't do anything wrong. That's what you grew up knowing as a young child in the church.

I'm beginning to recognize that it was all steps toward taking advantage. Kids just don't realize, because they don't know what sex is. They don't understand when someone's leading up to it. I think parents really need to talk with their children about it. Child sexual abuse is sick, but it's happening, so you have to deal with it.

After a while, Father Jim got more aggressive, more sexual. He started doing other stuff to me, like kissing and touching. He'd do it in his car or in our house when everyone was outside or busy. I had no clue what was going on, but it felt weird.

Then when I was ten I was sitting on his lap in the bathroom. He asked me to look for scars under his private parts. He pulled down his pants and had me look. He was masturbating while I was checking him for, so he said, scars. I told him, "Oh, no, I don't see anything," and stood up, and that's when he forced me to have oral sex with him.

When he was finished he buttoned up his pants and tucked his shirt back in. I started to walk out and he told me, "No, come back." He pulled me down on his lap again and said, "You can't tell anyone about this. If you tell anyone, God's going to hate you. God's going to hate your family. You're going to burn in hell and so is your family."

Being a little kid, having no clue what's going on, I was scared to death. Like, what if somebody finds out? This guy was a priest. I thought he must know what would happen if I told. I believed him. I didn't tell.

That coming weekend, Father Jim was supposed to pick me up to go to the shore with him. It was a three-day weekend, a holiday. And I thought to myself, "What's going to happen? If he takes me away, am I ever going to come back? I don't want to go. I don't want to do this stuff anymore."

I thought if I killed myself and it looked like an accident, nobody would find out. Then my family wouldn't burn in hell. So I planned to hold a steak knife to my heart and run into the wall.

But Father Jim never showed up that morning. He never did show up again. I had no clue what had happened. I thought he just forgot me.

Must have been a couple of weeks later, my mom and one of my older brothers were sitting at the dining room table with a man dressed in a nice business suit. They called me in from outside, where I was playing with my Matchbox cars. Mom asked me if anything strange ever happened with Father Jim, if he'd touched me in weird places. I got scared. I thought, "Oh, my God, they found out! That's it. I'm done for. We're all gonna burn in hell." So I denied it.

middle school

I was ten years old. Even after the abuse stopped, I was so worried about it, so confused, I started having migraine headaches and I couldn't sleep through the night. I had these nightmares every night. I'd wake up sweating and crying and wet the bed. That's actually one of the big symptoms of child sexual abuse. I wet the bed until I was twelve years old.

I didn't understand what had happened to me. The schools inform you on sexual diseases, drugs, and alcohol, which is good, but they need to hit a lot of other issues, too, like sexual abuse. They say that one out of every four children is sexually abused. In a class of twenty-four kids, there's a good chance that five or six are abused—or will be.

Because I didn't have that information I started thinking that what happened was my fault, that I did something to bring it on. Like I did something wrong or that I was gay.

When I started middle school and realized what sex was, that's when I really started having a problem with this. Everybody's trying to be the cool one. You know, "I kissed this girl" or "I did this with that girl." But my first kiss was with a man! What happened with Father Jim made me feel like a lesser person.

When I was about eleven years old I started smoking and drinking. It was an unconscious means of coping, but I didn't realize it then. Smoking cigarettes made me feel like, yeah, I was growing up, I was cool, I wasn't a little faggot like I thought I was.

In middle school, my life was hell. I felt I had not a friend in the world. I felt my family hated me. I didn't know what there was to live for. Like, I didn't understand how people could be happy. What was life? Why would you want to live?

Cigarettes, marijuana, and alcohol made me forget my worries, and I thought that was a good thing. I thought that was a great thing! Why would you *not* want to drink and smoke pot? From there, I thought I'd never do anything harder, but I started tripping off acid and 'shrooms and I started snorting coke. Life was a pitch-dark hell to me and doing drugs made me forget that. It made me feel happy. What I didn't realize was that at the same time it was causing me to have *more* problems emotionally, physically, and education-wise.

It wasn't until eighth grade that the drugs took effect emotionally. I was constantly fighting, always trying to prove that I was a real man, that I wasn't less than anyone else. When I got mad or upset, I'd cut myself with a box cutter. Cut my arms and legs. I don't know why, but at the time it felt good to do it. It was like I was getting rid of the emotional pain by feeling physical pain instead.

I got real suicidal. I took a bunch of pills that I found in the house. I went to bed and planned on never waking up again. It was either live in this hell or move on to the next one, because I knew if I died I'd go to hell. Father Jim told me so. It was just too much to take anymore.

I didn't die, but I got real sick. I didn't tell anyone what I'd done until just last year.

hero

In eighth grade I was really into writing. I was taking a creative writing and public speaking class. We had to write about our hero. I wrote about my brother because deep down inside I had this feeling he had stopped Father Jim from coming to pick me up. He was my hero for that.

So I wrote a story about my brother saving my life, saving me from jumping off a bridge. The teacher already had thoughts that I might be into drugs and alcohol, and now, seeing the suicidal stuff in my story, sent me to the school guidance counselor. The counselor called my parents and set up an appointment for me with a therapist.

I started going to the therapist and telling her about dreams I was having, about somebody chasing me through the woods, and I'd wake up sweating and crying and wet the bed. It was weird, it would happen over and over again. When I told her that, I totally disbelieved that this woman could help me. I never believed in her theory of being able to control your own dreams. I thought it was total bull crap. But it worked.

Her theory was to find out who was chasing me by turning around in the dream and then doing whatever I wanted, like punch him. It didn't work that way. I didn't turn around and shoot him like I wanted to. But I did wake up and see his face and that's when all the pieces just clicked together. I realized the connection between the sexual abuse and the drugs and everything.

So I told my therapist what happened between me and Father Jim. The therapist told my mom. On the ride home my mom said that the same thing had happened to my brother. That weekend when Father Jim was supposed to take me away, my brother had told my parents not to let me go. When they said there was no reason to keep me home, he said, "Yes, there is." And he told them—to protect me. That's why Father Jim never showed up that morning to pick me up. My brother really did save my life.

My parents had reported what my brother said to the church officials. It turned out that the guy in the suit who asked me those questions when I was ten was a church attorney.

This time we decided to go to the police department to file charges. I gave a deposition, told the detective most of what had happened. I didn't tell him the full details. I didn't tell about the oral sex or some of the ways that Father Jim had touched me, because I was embarrassed. I'm a guy and I was thirteen years old. I didn't want them to think I was gay. They didn't have enough to go on and they were busy with other cases. My family just wanted to hurry up and end it, so we settled with the church. The church paid me a large sum of money, and me and my parents had to sign a paper saying I would never talk about it to anyone. The church gave me money in trade for my voice.

I kept quiet for three years—until this past July. That period I kept quiet, I felt like the black sheep at school. I always had problems. It was hard, not being able to tell anyone what happened. A lot of kids didn't understand me. Sometimes, when you're in school, you see these kids that are misfits, these kids that are out there who nobody really takes a liking to, these drug addicts or bad apples. You say, "Ah, that kid's nothing but a piece of crap. That's just how he was raised." But if you look deeper into that person's life, you realize maybe there's something behind it. Maybe he needs help.

This past July I saw a couple of older guys on TV who were abused by priests, guys in their thirties and forties. That's when I realized I wasn't the only one. I'm not alone. And it just happened that these guys were from the same parish as me; they were all from south Jersey.

So I got hold of this group called SNAP, Survivors Network of those Abused by Priests. I started going to the meetings, met other people just like me. It was one of the biggest healing processes for me because—therapist, family, friends—no matter how much they want to help, people do not understand how you feel unless they have gone through it, too. These people became family to me. They knew exactly what I felt. They finished my sentences and I could finish theirs. They were men, women, all ages.

At seventeen, I was the youngest in the group. That was kind of hard, being the youngest. I didn't like the fact that everyone kept telling me how courageous I was for coming out at such a young age.

It's different for me than for them because there's so much more support for survivors now. Ten, twenty, thirty years ago, there were no support groups. When people spoke out then, no one wanted to believe it.

In ninth and tenth grade, I'd done some public speaking for PEP—that's Peer Education Program—where high school students who'd gone through drug and alcohol abuse went to talk at elementary schools. Last year, in eleventh grade, I took a whole year of classes in creative writing and public speaking.

When I got involved with SNAP, I decided I wanted to speak out like the older guys. Their reason for doing it is to try to change the church. I wanted to speak out to help other kids. People told me that if I spoke out I might lose the money, and I told myself, "If I help one kid—one kid—that'll be worth it."

SNAP set me up with a reporter from *The Philadelphia Inquirer* and she did a big exclusive on the front page of the Sunday paper. Two days later, we held a press conference.

from the heart

After that I started speaking in schools. A program called Services Empowering Rape Victims called me. They'd seen me in the newspaper and they asked, "Would you be interested in talking to a couple of people, maybe even giving a speech to a small group?"

So I got hooked up with them and did a speech at a high school in Camden. I walked in and I was the only white person in the room. I was like, "I can't believe I'm doing this," I was so nervous. When I got up to speak, they were all looking at me like, "Who the hell is this kid?"

I told them my story, that I'd been sexually abused. I let the words come from my heart, not a piece of paper. I said, "If you look at life as a road, it has these potholes, the heavy things that happen to you. As I see it, if you try to ignore them or cover them up, not take the time to really deal with them, you're liable to drive back over them and fall in. You've got to take care of them, fill them in, so they don't mess you up." I told them that if I'd never talked to anybody, I would have never gotten help. That's the number-one thing: get help.

When I got done with the speech, everybody stood up. Everybody was in tears and clapping. This one huge kid ran to the front of the room and picked me up and hugged me. It was just amazing. It made me feel so good that I could reach out to other kids and affect them so positively. I decided to do more.

Other teenagers can see that I'm a kid just like them, from an everyday town like theirs, and it hits home. That's when people realize that sexual abuse isn't just a story in a book or a scene in a movie. It's something that happens every single day to people like them.

After the newspaper interview and the press conference, so many kids called me and e-mailed me. People come up to me in public and say, "Hey, aren't you that kid? My friend needs help" or "I know someone who is being abused." Helping other people made me realize there is a purpose in life.

Once I started speaking out and helping people, I realized that this was what I wanted to do. Not for a living, because I'm going to be a pilot, but as my contribution. This is my little bit to make the world better.

out at school

When I spoke out, I thought every one of my friends was going to laugh at me. But 100 percent have been right there behind me. Anything I need, anytime I want to talk, they've been there for me. I have their total support.

But you don't have to talk to all your friends about everything. You don't have to get too much into details. It's hard to go into those segments of the past where you're not totally healed. The best person to do that with is a therapist.

When other kids at school found out about what happened to me, a lot of them didn't know how to act. Some people wanted to talk to me. Some kind of ignored me because they didn't know what to say. Some were just uncomfortable with the whole situation.

I remember walking through the hallway at school after the first newspaper article came out. It was my first year in a new school, so I didn't know everybody. I was walking behind this one kid and I heard him say, basically, "I'd have sex with a priest for that much money." Got me real upset, but then I told myself, "You knew people were going to have things to say about this. But the negative you get is nothing compared to the good that comes from speaking out." And it's true, talking about it brought me together with a lot of my friends. It made my life so much easier.

The guy who made that comment apologized to me later. I said, "Don't worry about it." If I hadn't been abused, if I'd just heard this story, I wouldn't know what to think either. I might be joking about it, too. But when people really look at what happened and get some insight, they are more understanding than you would ever think.

are you gay?

There's been a lot of questions from my friends like, "Are you still suicidal?" One friend even asked me if I was gay. And I had these thoughts, too: "If I had sex with a guy, does that mean I'm gay?" But I've found out I'm not gay, I just had these doubts inside me. That's been one of the hardest things to deal with. I mean, I was ten years old, and my introduction to sexuality was with an older male, someone I looked up to.

But being sexually abused by another male doesn't make you gay. It doesn't work that way. You are who you are.

There are so many different kinds of people in this world. One of my family members is gay and I have gay friends. Now I know it's not something to be embarrassed about or ashamed of. And being gay doesn't make someone a pedophile.

I still don't feel comfortable around older men. Maybe it's because I put my total trust and confidence in Father Jim and he took advantage of it. That kind of thing can affect your comfort level and your trust for a long time.

family

My family has been my biggest support. My brother who saved me is still my hero, and he says I'm his hero for speaking out. My parents have gone through so much for me. I think to this day they feel like they should have known, should have stopped it, and they blame themselves. I hate that so much. I wish there was something I could do to make them not feel like that, because there is no way they could have known. I mean, I hid it purposely for years.

When I was younger and being sexually abused and even after, before anyone found out about the abuse, I hated my parents. I hated my family. I didn't know why, I just did. I tried running away a couple of times. I beat the hell out of my little brothers and sisters, always fighting. I was horrible.

Once I started going to counseling and realized why I did it—that I was taking out my frustration and anger about the abuse on them—I stopped. My attitude totally changed. And their attitude toward me changed because they were able to understand why I'd been so horrible to them. That was a big thing to me, to have my family's support—even though I had treated them like crap in the past.

My relationship with my family has just grown enormously. We take time to listen to each other and really find out what's going on in each other's lives. If you would have told me when I was thirteen that my family would be my best friends, I would have told you, "No way." But now my family means the world to me. They love me to death and I'd take a bullet for any one of them.

faith

I believe in God. I still pray every day. I thank God for giving me life and everything in it. But I've lost my faith in the church. I don't know if I'll ever be able to step inside a Catholic church again. I tried to go back once but I couldn't even walk through the doors.

The church is supposed to be a representation of God, the place you go to find love, peace, and happiness. Instead, for me it represents the darkness in my life. It isn't just that I was abused by a priest, but because of the way the church tried to hide it.

There is someone in the church I totally respect. When I decided to speak out, I called and asked to talk with my bishop, Bishop Di-Marzio, one-on-one. It was hard to go in there and sit down face-to-face with someone from the church, but I wanted to tell him that I was choosing to speak out and that he could have the money back. He told me that the church was going to vacate confidentiality agreements. That meant I could keep the money. But, more important, he was really sincere about wanting things to change. He apologized that the abuse ever happened to me. It was the first time that anyone from the church really reached out to me.

A month later, I was down in Washington, D.C., with SNAP and other advocacy groups for the National Conference of Catholic Bishops. One night, we were handing out candles with a prayer for survivors on them, seeing if any of the bishops would take them. They were all walking past with their heads down, ignoring us and hopping on the bus. They had cops guarding them so we couldn't go near. The only one who took a candle was Bishop DiMarzio. He walked over to me in front of all those people. He said, "How you doing, Jonathan? I'll say a prayer for you." He's that kind of guy.

I believe that the church is going to change. It's going to change because of people like Bishop DiMarzio.

flying

I just found out I got into pilot school, the number-one aviation school in the country. I'm so excited. It's a big thing for me. I'm planning to earn every one of my pilot certifications and degrees, study aeronautical engineering, and one day hopefully fly a Lear jet for a private company.

My dream is to travel the whole world, writing, doing photography, and just enjoying life. I mean, there's a lot of things I want to do in the future. Eventually I want to have a family, settle down with a wife and kids—one or two kids. It's fun being from a big family, but to tell you the truth, I don't think I could handle one myself.

For now, I have my nieces and nephews. Angel is my pride and joy.

Kelly

THE RAPE DIDN'T DERAIL MY LIFE, but it did change me. It became the subject of my first film. It gave me a sense of empathy that is one of the strong points of my journalism career. As a newspaper reporter, a lot of what I'm asked to do is talk with people in crisis. I know what it is like to live through that floating, post-traumatic numbness. I know what it is like to testify in court.

Compared to many people who are sexually assaulted, I was really lucky. My family and friends were supportive. The whole justice system went extremely smoothly for me. The rapist was caught that day and he's in prison for life, so I don't ever have to fear that he'll come after me.

Everyone believed me—even I didn't think it was my fault. I mean, I was fourteen years old. A stranger with a weapon grabbed me off the street. Who would question my role in that?

kidnapped

The rape happened the week I graduated from eighth grade. We'd just moved. I was going to summer school at my new high school, taking

Health to get it out of the way. But my biggest priority that summer was making friends.

I wanted to know *someone* when I went into ninth grade in the fall. I didn't know anyone at my new school yet, but I had met some younger kids in the neighborhood. They showed me a shortcut around the back side of the school.

That morning I was walking alone, running a little bit late. I turned the corner and there was a man, sitting on the gymnasium steps.

He was quite a bit away, but I could tell he was looking at me funny. Something about him made me uncomfortable. I didn't listen to that voice inside that said, "Stop. Don't go there." Instead, I thought, "Isn't it rude to go out of your way to avoid someone?" and I kept walking toward him.

As I passed him, he stood up. Then he grabbed me from behind, around my neck. With his other hand, he showed me a knife and he said, "Don't scream."

I didn't scream. I didn't fight him. I just got into his station wagon.

Immediately, I started crying and breathing fast, hyperventilating. We had some conversation through my tears. I asked him where he was taking me and he said, "To the hills." He told me he had the knife by my side, basically reminding me not to try to fight him. I asked what he wanted and he said, "Just let me have my fun and I'll let you go."

At a stoplight, I tried to get the attention of the woman in the car next to us. He realized what I was doing and told me to look straight ahead.

We kept driving. I didn't know where. He took me up this winding canyon road. While he was driving he started touching me, my breasts, my vagina.

My heart was beating so fast it scared me. "I have a weak heart," I told him. "I'm afraid it will stop." I didn't really have a heart condition, but at the time it felt like it.

Eventually, he turned onto a dirt road. He drove up a hill and parked in a secluded area in the hills. He told me to get out of the car, take off all my clothes, and lie on this little square of carpet that he took out of the car. Then, basically, he started raping me.

I kept my eyes closed. I was like, "I'm NOT here. I'm NOT going through this." My brain checked out a little. You do whatever you can to not be fully aware. But I did say something about my heart again. I was afraid it was going to stop beating.

He stopped. I think he was losing his erection or something. Then he ejaculated on me.

"I'm going to do you a favor and let you go," he said. He told me I could get dressed.

It had never occurred to me that he wouldn't let me go. The possibility that he might kill me never entered my mind. I was operating on the assumption that I would do whatever he wanted, just to get this over with.

Voluntarily I said, "I won't tell anybody what happened."

He said, "Good. 'Cause if you do, I'll come back and kill you."

At the time, to me, that wasn't such a scary exchange. I said what I did to reassure him so I could get away. And he said what he was supposed to, in return. I knew that as soon as he left I was going to a police station—but I wasn't going to tell him that.

Instead, I asked if I could get my schoolbooks out of the car. I didn't want to get in trouble for not having my Health book.

When he drove off, I was sitting on the ground behind the car, tying my shoes. I looked up and saw the car's license plate. It was right in front of me. I thought, "If they're going to catch him, I have to re-member this." I started repeating the letters and numbers in my head.

Then I realized I had paper and pencils with my books, so I wrote it down.

I waited long enough for him to drive back down the hill, then I ran the same way, to the paved road. There was still some morning-commute traffic. I waved my arms at the passing cars, yelling and cry-ing. A lot of cars passed me and I thought, "If he was chasing me out here, would anyone even stop to help me?"

Finally, a man in a green truck stopped. I ran over to him. "Some-one tried to rape me." I didn't realize then that what happened really was rape. "Will you take me to the police station?"

Normally, I would never have done something like that, but under the circumstances I didn't hesitate. The man had this dad-like quality, kind and reassuring. He told me his name and showed me his work badge so I would know he was who he claimed to be. He took me to a nearby fire station and they called the police.

evidence

The first police officer to arrive wanted me to go back to the scene im-mediately. He drove me to the base of the dirt road and we walked back up it together. I showed him my footprints, the tire tracks, and where the car was parked. Then he brought me back to the fire sta-tion; my parents were waiting for me there.

When I walked into the room, I was so relieved to see my mom and dad. And yet, it was hard, too. They were so obviously worried. I ended up trying to reassure them that I was okay.

I don't remember what my mom said. I just remember that she

hugged me and that she was really frazzled that whole day. When my mom gets upset, she goes into crisis mode—she focuses on the things, physical things, that need to get done.

There are a lot of time-sensitive aspects to a rape case. The police need to get physical evidence as soon as they can. We were about to drive to the hospital, for the medical exam, when we learned that the police actually caught the guy.

They had run a check on his license plate, gotten his address, and gone to see if he was home. When he opened the door, he said, "Yeah, it was me."

So, instead of having a formal police lineup for me to identify him, they drove me by his house in an unmarked police car. Raymond Barthlett was standing outside in handcuffs. I confirmed that he was the man who did it. Then we drove to the hospital.

I'd never had a gynecological exam before, but my mom had, of course. She stayed with me. The nurse who did it was so nice and so careful. There were certain things she had to do, like pluck five pubic hairs and cut five pubic hairs. It's weird, but they need them for the rape kit—for evidence. This poor nurse kept saying, "I'm really sorry I have to do this." And I'm like, "It's okay," reassuring her.

The nurse used a scanner, sort of like a black light, to see where his body fluids were. She turned the room lights out and waved the scanner over me. My mom was horrified because you could see there was dried semen glowing purple all over my front. But I thought it was pretty cool. I was like, "Wow, they can actually do that!" I was fixating on the interesting aspects of the exam. Maybe that's what you do to get through things like that.

Then I went home and took a shower. My older sister told me she was very sorry about what happened to me. The next day we had this big party at our house because it was her high school graduation.

That's the way my family is. After something bad happens, you pull yourself together and carry on. We couldn't cancel the party. Everyone was coming from our old town because that's where my sister and her friends had just graduated. My eighth-grade boyfriend came, too. He was a good guy. I told him everything that happened, or nearly everything. That was a lot to lay on someone, but he was really sweet.

The nurse who did the rape exam had asked me if I kept a journal. In fifth grade I decided that I wanted to be a writer, so I kept one even though I didn't always write in it. She said, "It would be a good thing for you to go home and write down what you remember while it's still fresh." The day after the party, I wrote a detailed description in my journal. It was so detailed that years later I used it when I made the film about the rape.

Within three or four days the police wanted me to come in and write a witness report. I wrote a good fifteen pages. The district attorney had a DNA match from the rape exam and a witness who hadn't lost her cool—I remembered everything down to the color of Barthlett's eyes. They had all the evidence they needed to convict him. I think that's why he agreed to plead guilty.

Later he was sentenced to twenty years in prison. I calculated that with good behavior, the earliest he could get out was when I was twenty-four, so it was something I could push off into the future.

that summer

The rape happened on a Friday. The party was on Saturday. On Monday my parents drove me to school. From then on they always drove me and my younger sister to school. Quietly, without a lot of fanfare, they did things to make us all feel more comfortable, like installing a security system in our home.

The week after the rape, I wrote in my diary, "I think I'm okay now." I kept really busy. I was in summer athletics and I spent time at the gym. Later my family went on vacation to Idaho. It was a summer full of distracting activities. For me that helped. But looking back, I realize that I was also experiencing post-traumatic stress. I felt jumpy, uncomfortable, sometimes kind of numb.

One day, shortly after the assault, my mom had to run some errands and my sister went with her. They asked if I wanted to come and I said, "No, I want to stay home. I'll be fine." They left and I was alone for the first time since the rape. I got really freaked out. It was that heart-pounding, stomach-sinking kind of fear.

The nurse at the hospital had given me a card with the phone number for the rape crisis center. She said, "Don't be shy about calling them." She told me that it wasn't silly or weak or irrational to reach out and ask for help when you need it.

So I called and talked to a counselor. I was mad at myself for feeling scared because I've always been an independent person and I usually like spending time alone. She helped me see that it was reasonable to be upset, that I wasn't a freak for feeling vulnerable.

My parents told my teacher and the principal about the rape. My mom wanted to make sure I didn't get penalized for missing class and my dad wanted the school to tighten their security. Otherwise, my mom's approach was "I don't want people to know." I think my parents were concerned that I might be labeled as "the one who was raped." They wanted it to be on my terms who knew. It was always up to me who I told.

I also went to some counseling that summer, so I had that private time, talking with a professional. The state paid for it through the Victim Assistance program because I had reported the rape.

friends

My freshman year of high school would have been hard no matter what. You are trying to make friends and figure out where your place

is. I was trying out for sports, too. On top of that, I was new and I'd had this really horrible experience in the summer.

There were times when I just wanted to hole up. It was very tempting to wear baggy clothes and sit around the house and— you know—be locked up inside.

You do have to slog through the tears and the stress. Cry and get it out of your system and cry again. But what worked for me was to also keep doing the other things I needed to do. Go to school. Try to make friends. Get involved. Go out and practice with the team. Physical exercise seemed to help me clear my head.

Pretty early on I found new friends, people who were in a lot of my classes and were very much like me—good at school and into sports. I was pretty open with them about the rape. I found a sense of support from that. Mostly it was just the fact that they listened, but sometimes they knew someone else who had been through something similar.

I could talk openly with almost everyone else I was close to but my parents. In my family, we don't talk about emotions a lot. I knew that this subject was painfully hard for them. It seemed like the safest way to respect their feelings was to not bring it up.

During my freshman year, I didn't really date anyone. I wasn't ready yet. I still had things I wanted to work out on my own.

dating

A lot of dating is figuring out who you want to be with. I realized that it was important to me to find someone who was a friend first, someone I could talk things over with.

My mom was really worried that I would be frigid sexually. She was concerned that I would be afraid of men, or not willing to open up in a relationship and establish a true partnership, like she has with my dad. Before the rape she was fairly open about sex. She would say, "When two people are married, sex is something wonderful and shared."

After I started dating, there was this one boy. We'd only gone on three dates, but it seemed like it might get serious. My mom cornered me and said, "Have you kissed him yet?" And I hadn't. Everyone else's mother was worried they'd get pregnant and my mother was rooting for me to start kissing!

Later she asked if I'd told a boy I was dating about what happened to me. He was a really nice guy, a friend, and she said, "I think you can trust him. It would be a good thing." I finally worked up the courage and told him the whole story one night. He burst out and told me that it had happened to him, too. When he was a small child a stranger had grabbed him and raped him and was never caught. That blew me away. All the time I was freaking out about telling him and he understood completely.

I began to feel that until people knew what happened to me, they didn't really know me, because the rape was such a defining moment in my life. The act of telling someone is an act of trust—it is letting someone in.

In college, I dated Jason—he's my husband now—only a couple of weeks before I told him. Nothing that bad had ever happened in his life. He was so surprised, he found it overwhelming. Maybe I should have waited, but what I have found is that if you give people the chance, 99.5 percent of the time they rise to the occasion.

sex

A really strong, solid man knows that sex isn't about trying to get something over on the other person. With Jason, as we got more intimate, he made sure that I was comfortable, that we could talk about anything, including things that might remind me of the rape. Like me, he wants our intimacy to be pleasurable, shared—not scary or painful.

You have to be willing to ask each other, "What's this like for you? How do you feel?" And really listen. And you have to speak up for yourself as well.

It's not just sex, but everything in the relationship. One time I was washing dishes and Jason thought it would be funny to come up behind me and grab me. I was so scared. For me, it was like being grabbed by the rapist. I said, "Don't ever do that again!" I knew he didn't mean to scare me, but he needed to know that for me it wasn't funny.

I waited a long time to have sex. And I'm glad I did. When it came on my terms—when I decided I was ready—I found that sex was a really positive experience.

murder

In college, I went to Zimbabwe, in Africa, for a semester to study the Shona language and culture. When I got back, my mom asked me to go with her on a walk.

As we walked, she told me that the district attorney's office called while I was out of the country. They were going to charge Raymond Barthlett with the murder of a fourteen-year-old girl who had died the year before I was abducted.

"You mean there was another girl? He killed her?" I remember that everything seemed to slow down. All these thoughts went through my head. "Who was she? Does she look like me? Why am I alive?"

Like me, Wendy Osborn had been kidnapped on the way to school. She was taken into the same hills as I was, where she was raped and then strangled. Seven years later, someone in the crime lab matched Barthlett's DNA from my rape with the samples taken from Wendy's body. The district attorney wanted me to testify at the murder trial. I was very willing to help.

For the first time in years, my mom and I talked openly about the rape. It was good. I asked, "Why didn't you ever talk with me like this before?" She said, "You didn't want me to." I said, "What are you talking about? I thought you were afraid." "No," she told me. "There was this one time when I was trying to get you to talk about it, and you looked at me and said, 'I don't ever want to talk about this again, period.' And I respected that."

I don't remember saying that, but I probably did. That's just the kind of thing I would have said. And a part of me knew all along that if I really needed to, I could have talked with my parents.

It took a whole year before Barthlett came to trial. When you testify in court you don't get to watch the trial. On the day I testified the prosecutors kept me in this little room until the moment I was called to the stand.

I walked in and faced Raymond Barthlett for the first time since the rape. He seemed smaller than I remembered and almost pathetic.

Testifying at the trial was totally nerve-racking. But there is something incredibly valuable about getting to tell your story in your own words in an officially sanctioned room where the person who hurt you has to listen to you and so does everybody else.

The jury found him guilty. He was sentenced to life in prison for Wendy's murder.

Afterward, one of the jurors said that I was both strong and lucky. I don't know why Wendy didn't make it and I did. I don't think it was because I did anything better than she did. I think it is just the luck of how things played out. But it's hard to deal with. When you survive and someone else doesn't, you can feel guilty, which I did.

I am a writer, that's what I do. There was one point when I was stuck. All I could write about was the rape. I was getting frustrated with myself because I felt like, this happened so long ago, can't I get over this? I mentioned this to one of my writer friends and she said, "If the rape is what you need to write about, just write about it until you don't need to anymore. Then you can move on to the next thing."

It was perfect advice, so clear and obvious. Don't fight what you need to do. Your feelings aren't wrong. Do what you have to do and in time you'll get past it.

After college, I went to journalism school to become a professional writer—a print journalist. But I thought it would be fun to learn about making documentaries for TV. So I took classes to learn how to work the camera and do the TV-production side. Everyone in the second-year documentary class had to write film proposals and then make a film.

I wanted to tell the story of Wendy's disappearance and how the murder was solved. But I wanted the story to be about more than the crime itself. What interested me was the larger universe of all the people it affected. What was it like for my parents? For the Osborns?

My professor said, "This is an amazing idea. My only question for you is if you want this to be your first film."

For me, though, it went back to the whole thing with my writing. I couldn't do anything else until I told this story. Making the film was the excuse I needed to ask the questions that—for whatever reason— I felt I couldn't ask before.

This was also a good time to make it because I had so much support. The class was collaborative. We worked as crews on each other's films, we gave each other feedback. When I interviewed my parents, two friends came with me to run the big camera and lights.

My mom spent the first twenty minutes of our interview speaking about me in the third person. She'd say, "My daughter was kidnapped," and I'd say, "Mom, people will know it's me interviewing my own mother, so you can just say 'you.'"

Finally it clicked and she started talking to me instead of the camera. When she relaxed, she became more herself. For the first time I learned that she had battled hard to get the morning-after pill for me.

When I asked my dad what it was like to see me testify at the trial, he told me how my siblings reacted. I think that reflects his role in our family. He was the one who had to hold it together, go to court, speak for the family, comfort his wife, and make his children feel safe.

"But what was it like for *you*?" I asked.

"Like it is now," he said, choking up. "Difficult." Tears spilled out of his eyes. "As a parent you think you can protect your kids and look out for them. You can't always do that."

Off camera I was crying, too. It was the first time I heard how my father felt about the rape. It was one of the few times I've seen him cry.

The Osborns were my last interview. We had met briefly at the trial, after my testimony. At that time Mr. Osborn had told me not to feel guilty. But I felt bad that I was alive when they'd lost their daughter. You can't help but feel like a source of pain. It would be totally reasonable for them to wonder, "Why couldn't it have been Wendy who lived?"

It was two weeks before my wedding when my classmates and I finally drove to their house. I felt awkward at first. We were still learning how to make a film, so we made a big mess trying to set up the cameras. The Osborns were so kind to me. They said, "Just call us when you're ready."

Interviewing them, I wore the shield of the filmmaker. I had my list of questions. Under what other circumstances could I have asked things like, "What was it like to see me at the trial?"

Mr. Osborn said that the only time he cried during the trial was after I testified, when we met in the hall for a few moments and then I turned and walked away.

"I have no desire to make you trade places with my daughter," he told me in the interview. "But I wish she had survived."

Then he said, "It's good to see you all grown up. Have a good wedding."

The first time I showed the unedited tapes, the class was stunned. I couldn't stop crying. Then they came over and comforted me. I dragged my poor classmates through the whole process!

When you edit, you see the same scene over and over and over again. There was a moment when I stopped thinking about my personal story and switched over to thinking about how the viewer was going to see things. The emotion came out of it a bit and it wasn't so upsetting.

Making the film helped me be more forgiving. Of myself, for surviving. Of my parents, for the difficulty they had talking about the rape. Clearly, when I put it all together, my parents were incredibly supportive and incredibly good parents.

Debbie—the adviser who helped me edit the film—said, "This is going to save you years of therapy."

Making and showing the film is totally outing myself as a rape survivor. I don't feel stigmatized at all, but sometimes it's a bit weird to think that for some people, this is all they know about me. The rape

was literally one hour out of my life. I'm not belittling that. But there is a lot more to who I am.

In the big, big picture, I have a good life. I love my job as a reporter—it allows me to indulge my curiosity and to write every day. I'm married to a wonderful man. We just bought a house and we are thinking about starting a family.

At this point in my life, if I could wish the rape away, I don't think I would. I like the person I am now and who I am has been influenced by the rape. It forced me to be strong, to get through it all. If I were to wish that experience away, I might be wishing away the source of my strength.

• • •

Forever Fourteen, Kelly St. John's documentary about the death of Wendy Osborn, was aired on the PBS program "Life 101" and received a 2002 Emmy Award from the Academy of Television Arts and Sciences.

Sheena

I DIDN'T EVEN WANT TO BABYSIT THAT NIGHT. One of my distant cousins, who's a lot older than me, wanted me to stay with his kids so he and his girlfriend could go to a wedding social here on the reserve. My mom wanted to go out, too, and I didn't want to be bored at my cousin's house, so I brought my little sisters with me. It was last year, when I was fifteen and my sisters were eight and nine years old.

assault

In the middle of the night, my cousin came home. I was asleep on the couch and my sisters were sleeping on the floor nearby. He leaned over me and put his hand here, on my chest. I thought I was just dreaming. Then his hand went lower and I woke up. I saw his hand and grabbed it.

He was drunk. He said, "What? Are you scared?" and I said, "No. Quit it!"

I still thought I might be asleep, so I turned over and curled up with my face to the back of the couch.

But he put his hand on me again, lower down; I don't feel comfortable saying exactly where. He was like, "You don't need to be scared.

You don't need to be shy. I know you want this," or something like that. Then I knew I was awake and this was really happening to me.

I had to think fast. He had me by the wrist and pulled me up off the couch. As I got up, I kicked hard at my sister. I didn't want to hurt her but I wanted to wake her up. I didn't want to be alone with him.

My cousin pulled me into his bedroom and onto his bed. He took his shirt off; underneath he had on a muscle shirt. He told me to rub his back, but I didn't want to. Then he pulled me over toward him. He held me down and put one leg over me.

"My sister is up," I told him, but he didn't stop. I pushed him, I tried hard to get up, and then I just went stiff.

Now I could see both my little sisters through the open door. "My sisters are coming," I told him. He loosened his grip and I fought my way back up.

He said, "Tell them to go back to bed." But I didn't want to say that! I told him to go find his girlfriend; she could come sleep with him.

My sisters were watching him now. He was angry but he got up and left.

that night

As soon as he stepped out of the house, I started crying. I was so scared. My sisters grabbed me and held on to me and cried, too. We never thought this cousin, of all people, would do something like that.

We were afraid to stay, because what if he came back and was more violent? We were afraid to leave, because what if he caught us outside? Everyone was at the wedding and I didn't know how to reach my mom.

One of my little sisters grabbed a broom. She was going to hit him if he came back. I told my sisters that if he did come back, we should pretend that Mom phoned to tell us to go home. We were not going to stay in his house with him.

He did come back, so we left right away.

At home, I was still crying. I felt disgusted, like I had his germs on me and I couldn't wash them off. My sisters went to bed. My mom hadn't come home yet. I thought about one of my aunts. When she was a girl, something like this happened to her and no one believed her. What if no one believed me?

I went out the back door and stood on the steps. So many bad things had happened to me and I didn't know why. When I was two or three years old, a man abused me sexually. My mom and granny got help for me right away, but what he did was so bad, I had to stay in the hospital for days. I don't want to say more than that about it because it still really upsets me.

My mom tries so hard to make a good home for my sisters, my brother, and me. We've moved to different cities in Canada so she can find work, but we always end up coming back to the reserve where most of our family lives. Like a lot of people here, she struggles with drugs and alcohol. Some of the men in her life have not been good to her.

That night, I had no hope. I felt like my life was so hard, I wanted to kill myself. There's a big rock right next to the tree in our backyard and I knew where there was a rope. I prayed to God that I might have a better life than this one. "I don't deserve this," I said.

Then I saw my sisters' faces through the window. They were looking at me and crying so hard. I had this sudden thought: "If I kill myself tonight, how will that make my sisters feel?" I couldn't do that to them.

That was the second time that night my sisters saved me. Today I can't say thank you enough to them.

aftermath

My mom, she taught us that if anybody was to touch us where we didn't want to be touched, to tell her right away. So the next morning when she got home I told her. She freaked.

"Are you sure?" she kept asking me, like she couldn't believe what I was saying, like it was the last thing she wanted to hear.

I kept saying, "Yes!" Then Mom grabbed me and hugged me. She told me she didn't want her daughters to go through that. She was furious with my cousin.

We went down to my granny's house. She told my mom to talk to Lena, the director at Community Holistic Circle Healing, and to my Auntie Jane, who works there, too, because they both deal with sexual assault. CHCH is a program based on our traditional Ojibway healing, as well as modern counseling. Jane was my CHCH worker when I was abused as a little girl, and ever since then we've spent a lot of time together. She's not really my aunt but I call her Auntie because we're so close.

So that day after it happened, Lena picked up my mom and me. We drove around and we talked about what we were going to do. Lena told me I should charge him. Well, I was going to do that anyway. We talked about having a meeting, but what I wanted to do most was to get off the reserve for a week at least and think.

First, though, we had a healing circle.

They hold circles at Child and Family Services. It's part of their program for victims of sexual abuse and for offenders. There are all kinds of healing circles. Mine was a sharing circle.

That first circle I attended, I was mad. I didn't want to talk in front of everybody. The only reason I did it was because Auntie Jane and the others wanted me to do it. I just wanted to get it over with so I could go home.

Auntie Jane called the circle. My family came, and so did the people here who were trying to help us. It started with smudging and prayer. Smudging is when a leader goes around the circle and brushes sweet grass smoke over you. The smoke smells tangy and sweet. It purifies you and helps you get ready. After that, each person has a turn to talk. It started with me.

I had to tell what happened. That was hard, I was crying so much. And I didn't like everybody looking at me.

Then it was my sisters' turn. They told what happened. What my sisters had seen I didn't want them to see in their whole lives. Even though I didn't get raped, they're scared to grow up now, scared of men. If I hadn't asked them to come with me so I wouldn't be bored, they would have been spared that.

When my little brother talked, he said he wanted to grow up and become a cop so he could make sure that my cousin does time. His face and his eyes got all watery, and I was really shocked by how angry he was. I felt protected by my brother even though he's only thirteen.

When my mom talked, I found out that she blamed herself for what had happened. I didn't want to babysit that night because I was over at my friend Candina's house, but Mom got mad and made me go. Mom blames herself, she still does. "But you can't," I tell her. "How could you know what was going to happen?"

The circle ended after everyone had a chance to talk, including Auntie Jane and the others. We all stood up and held hands and said a prayer.

People in the circle all said things like, "I'm sorry about what happened to you." But afterward I thought, "No matter how many sorry's I hear, it's not going to bring back the trust I lost!" I was still angry.

in winnipeg

Afterward I went down to Winnipeg with my mom for a week so I could just get away and think. Winnipeg is about three hours away and it's the only big city in Manitoba. We've lived there several times and we have a lot of family and friends down there.

One of the CHCH workers drove us to Winnipeg. On the way, we stopped in Pine Falls to make a police report. Charging my cousin wasn't that hard to do. I didn't want to talk to a stranger about what had happened, but I know most of the cops. It isn't like the city up here. There are so few people that we all pretty much know each other.

I wanted my cousin to do time for what he did. The cops asked me if I wanted him to get help and I said, "Yes!" because he really needs it if he does things like that. I mean, he's so messed up.

Something happened in Winnipeg that hurt me more. We were staying with another aunt. Her boyfriend asked me if I fought back. You always think, "If something like that happens to me, I'd kick his ass. No one can mess with me!" But when it really happens to you,

you're like, your brain freezes, you panic so much. You do the best you can, but you can't always stop what's happening. When her boyfriend asked me that, I was like, "Well, *yeah,* I fought back." But it made me feel bad that he would question me like that.

back at school

Our school has about three hundred students—and that's from nursery through grade twelve. There are seventeen people in my grade. The kids come from six different Native towns around here, on and off the reserve. Everyone knows everybody else's business. That's why I don't want to go with any of the guys from around here. It's too close!

When I came back to school everybody was just staring at me. I was afraid they'd start asking me questions that would bring up bad memories. I felt like quitting, like running away.

It was scary to face other people. My cousin's family lives all around here. His brother is the boys' volleyball coach and our teams travel together to games. What if the coach was angry with me for charging his brother?

As it turned out, the coach was really kind to me. Still, I dropped out of sports and a lot of other things, too. I dropped out because I felt like the refs were looking at me in a sexual way. Usually I hang around with guy friends, but I backed away from them, too. And I wanted to quit school because most of my teachers were men. When they asked me to stay after class, I got scared. I wouldn't stay.

I couldn't stop crying, not even at school. The only people I could talk to were a few close friends. But when I started to talk to one of my best friends about it, she got so mad she wanted to pound his face.

I didn't want her being angry, so I didn't tell her any more. When I'd see a boy and girl holding hands it reminded me of my cousin grabbing my wrist. I'd think, "Is he forcing her?" and then I'd start crying again.

I felt like my cousin had taken something away from me, the trust I had in other people. I wasn't able to trust anyone, not even my uncles. I felt like he took my heart away and I could never get it back.

second circle

Before I had to go to court, we had a second circle. After the first one, I didn't want to do a circle again, but I told myself that I needed to go to one more so I would know what it was all about.

Auntie Jane called it at her house. At that second circle there was just my mom, my sisters, Auntie Jane, and a woman who had been abused by her uncle.

This circle was different. We talked less about what happened and more about our feelings.

That healing circle cleared me; it gave me courage to talk to people, to tell them how I felt, and to know that it wasn't just me these things happened to. After that, I could talk with my principal and vice-principal. I explained why I didn't want to stay with my teachers after school and they understood. I started talking with younger kids about what I had experienced and how they could protect themselves.

Since then, I've talked about sexual abuse with many other people. If I hadn't gone to that second circle, I probably wouldn't be able to tell you my story now.

At home, my mom has us do sharing circles with just our family. We begin with a prayer. Then we take turns talking and everybody else listens. We talk about how our lives are going and how we are feeling. My mom always asks if I'm okay. Then we close with a prayer. Those sharing circles feed my heart.

the sentence

Just before he was to go to trial, my cousin pleaded guilty. I didn't have to say anything at the sentencing hearing; I just had to show up, sit there in the crowd, and listen. Auntie Jane and my mom came with me.

I gave my victim-impact statement to the attorney and she read it out loud. The judge also read the statement I gave when I charged my cousin. I had told the cops that he'd been drinking. The judge read that and said that alcohol was not an excuse.

The cops told the judge that I wanted my cousin to get help. Instead of sending him to jail, the judge sent him back here. That wasn't what I wanted. I wanted him to go to jail *and* get help.

Instead, he gets to live at home. He has to stay away from me. He has to go through the healing circle program here, near where I live. That means for five years he has to take counseling every week and be in offender circles. They work on why they offended and how to stop themselves from doing it again. The whole community is supposed to keep an eye on them. Sometimes, an offender and his victims sit in the same circle, so the victims can say how they feel and the offender can say he's sorry.

But I don't want to sit in a circle with the cousin who did this to me. I don't want to be anywhere near him. I hate him. I never used to say that word, but now I do, I hate him so much.

When he didn't get time, I started crying again. I got scared he'd do something else to me. He's supposed to stay away from me, but what if I met him on the road around here? Would he beat me up?

I started sleeping more. I stopped thinking about sports. Everybody thought I was crazy because usually I'm the one who wants to get a game going at recess. I stopped fixing my hair. I didn't tell anyone, but I was thinking about suicide a lot.

My mom could see the difference in me. She knew something was up. She asked me what was wrong. But every time I tried to tell her I was feeling suicidal, she'd ask me why and I didn't want to explain it.

I was having flashbacks. I could see more and more of all the bad things that had happened to me. I was reliving the sexual assault that happened when I was really little. And the violence that I saw, the beatings that my mom took. She'd wear something that she wore when I was younger and it would trigger those bad memories. Or I'd see my sisters' faces and remember how scared we'd been that night at my cousin's house.

My mom stands by us, but she was upset about her own problems. My sisters and I were arguing over little things. I'd get so mad, I'd want to beat them up. I didn't, but I'd say mean things. We were all having a hard time.

I asked myself, "Why did all these bad things happen to us?" It just seemed like too much. I didn't care about life anymore. I wanted the hurting to end.

When I felt that way, I started acting like a daredevil and a tough girl. I talked back to my teacher. I'd go out and do ramps with four-wheelers, really crazy stuff. I ended up at the hospital twice from quad accidents. I don't know why I did those things. They didn't make me feel better. I felt depressed when I did them. I just didn't care if I lived or died.

My friends and my mom and my granny all tried to smarten me up. I did talk with them and Auntie Jane. My friends would come over. They told me that I'd been through enough, that they wanted me to have fun now. They'd take me over to their houses for sleep-overs. They got me out of the house. I just kind of went along.

sports

Ever since fourth grade I've wanted to be a basketball player. I played all the way through grade school. Whenever I play I feel so happy and free. I love that sport. Then, when I was in eighth grade, some girls from the high school team got into a fight with girls from another team. The school canceled girls' basketball for two years.

I'd waited so long to play basketball. Now I was starting grade ten and we were getting our team back. My friends asked if I was going to play, but I said no.

Our first sport in the fall is volleyball. A lot of my friends were on the team, so I came to watch them.

My friends were having so much fun; I wanted to join them again. For volleyball, there aren't so many spectators. It was a chance to build up slowly and get used to being around the refs and coaches again. It turned out to be a good season for us. Our girls' volleyball team came in second in the north.

When the basketball season started I did go out for the team. Our first game was the first home game in two years, so all these people came to watch. A whole bunch of boys from the visiting school were

there, too. I kept telling myself, "They can think what they want about my personal problems. I want to play."

At first, I felt really, really weird because so many people were looking at me. But I started getting used to it during that game, which we won. Now I feel comfortable around guys again. It's a big change.

In basketball this year we had a lot of challenges. Varsity and juniors play together, but still there were only six of us on the team. That means only one sub. I play forward. This year I learned to shoot three-pointers. It's a long shot. The basket looks so small from back there. The first time I shot a three-pointer during a game I was like, "Whoa! It went in!"

The bus was especially fun, going to games and coming home. We had games in Pine Falls, about an hour from here. We came in third and we were happy because it was our first year. Now that people have seen us play, the team will grow.

The school only lets you play basketball if you get good grades. So this year I worked harder on my schoolwork and got my grades up. I hope to earn a Governor General's Award for high marks. Maybe I'll even be valedictorian.

Now I'm training for track and field. I go out for running. There are trails through the bush that make a circle around my community.

Every day I run around the town twice and then twice again in the evening. When I'm trying to beat my time, I'll think of something that makes me angry, like what my cousin did, and I run a whole lot faster.

When I got back into team sports, I started being more active around all my friends. But it was my friends from sports who kept me going. They helped me to see life differently, to see it for the gift it is. To see that God gave us one life to live and we should live it to the fullest.

struggles

Even though good things are happening, there have been times this year when I felt suicidal again. Once, I wrote my friends a three-page letter. I told them how bad I felt, that I didn't want to live and that they should not blame themselves. I got a lot of anger out writing that letter. After I gave it to them they all came and talked to me. They smartened me up. They said things like, "How do you think we'd feel? Don't do this to us." I was like, "I don't want to hurt you, but I don't want to keep hurting either."

When I get depressed like that, it feels like suicide is the only way out, but that isn't true.

There are things I can do to help myself. I get out more. And by that I don't mean partying or drinking, which is what a lot of people do around here. I don't do that or smoke either. I like to go to these cliffs overlooking the lake. It's a place where I can talk and pray out loud without anybody hearing me. Sometimes I scream if I'm really mad.

I spend more time doing things with my friends, like watching movies, playing soccer in the snow, or just hanging out. Right now we're planning a hockey tournament for younger kids and giving a dance class after school.

I love dancing. I do all kinds—hip-hop, square dancing, powwow dancing. We have dances at school and I've missed only one since sixth grade. My friends say I'm rich because I always have money to go to dances, but that's only because I babysit and save up. I'll never get tired of dancing, not even if I'm fifty-four.

Talking with Auntie Jane helps me, too. And I pray to God. I ask Him to make me strong enough to live life to the fullest, to not give up and commit suicide. So far it's worked!

strengths

I am full Indian, a Native person. My beliefs are both Christian and traditional.

My sister and I drum sing; that's like a prayer to the Creator, giving thanks for the earth. The guys drum and the girls sing at ceremonies and at powwows. I'm learning to be a jingle dancer for powwows, too. When I dance I feel free and full of courage.

Family is very im-

portant to me. From my granny and my mom I am learning Ojibwa, my Native language. I'm so proud of my brother; he's the youngest left-handed fiddler in Manitoba. My sisters like to dream about the future, but I tell them to start doing what they love now. One of my sisters wants to be a singer, so I encourage her to practice and get over her shyness.

And now there's baby Jacob. He's my heartbeat, my reason for living.

Jacob's dad is my mother's brother. He and his family live across the road from us. When Jacob's mom brought him home from the hospital, he just took my heart. I started hanging out over there all the time. I even taught him to crawl.

In a few weeks, I'm going to be his godmother. I can't wait. We'll all go to the Catholic church and stand in a circle while he gets baptized. I have to promise that I'll always take care of him and teach him about God and the traditional ways. After the ceremony we'll have a big feast.

I want to see Jacob grow up. I want to make his dreams come true.

the future

Once, I was shooting baskets outside of the school just for fun. This really, really tall guy came by and watched me. I found out later that he played for a team in Winnipeg. He came up to me and asked me how I liked the game.

I told him that I've loved it ever since I started playing in fourth grade. And I told him how in my very first game I didn't realize that the teams traded sides at halftime. I got so excited when we started to play the second half that I made a basket for the other team. He laughed and then he said, "You know, you're going to be a really good basketball player." I want to prove him right.

My dream is to play for the WNBA. But first, I want to go to college at the University of North Dakota because they have such a good women's team. I want to play for them, then go on to play professionally.

I'll probably study choreography, too. And maybe someday I'll be a gym teacher or a police officer.

The most important thing I want to say to people is this: if you've been abused or assaulted, hold on. And no matter how bad you feel, don't kill yourself. One way or another, the person who did it will get payback. Even if they don't, you've got the rest of your own life to live.

Oh, yes, and one other thing. In my aunties' day, people used to keep these things secret. But it's different now. I didn't want to tell anybody when it happened to me either, but I did. Once people know, you don't have to hide your feelings. You can start to get back your strength.

Tammy

WHEN I WAS FIFTEEN AND MY SISTER WAS FOURTEEN I finally asked her if my stepdad was messing with her, too. We were staying at his house and the two of us were sitting in the backyard talking. I asked, "Does he molest you?"

It took her a minute to answer me. Then she said, "Yes."

I'm so glad she told me. I don't know what I would have done if she said it hadn't happened to her, too. Why did I ask her? I got tired of feeling so bad. I really couldn't handle it anymore.

weekends

I've had three different fathers. My real father walked out when I was about six months old. For a while, he visited me, maybe once every three years or so. When I was thirteen, he told me he didn't love me and he never wanted to see me again. That hurt a lot.

The man I call my stepdad was my first stepfather. He stepped up to the plate when I was a baby and married my mom after my real father left us. He and my mom had three more kids together, then they divorced. Even after the divorce, he was like a father to me.

Now my mom is married to Michael. He's cool.

All of us kids used to go to my stepdad's house on the weekends. When he wasn't messing around with us, he could be really nice. He was fun, especially around birthdays.

But then he'd do stuff like mess with my privates. He told me he could do more with me because I wasn't his own kid. I don't know when it started, but I was little. When I was around thirteen, my sister and I were taking a bubble bath. He told my sister to go out and play with the rest of the kids. When she left, he got undressed and got in the bathtub with me. What he did then hurt really bad.

Later, he got me drunk so he could have his way with me. When you're under the influence of alcohol, it's kind of hard to tell what's going on. He told me that if I was going to smoke pot I should do it with him. One time when he got me drunk, I passed out and I woke up with my clothes off. I'm like, "Okay, that's weird because I *know* I did not take my clothes off myself." It freaked me out.

coping

What my stepdad was doing to me made me feel like I was no good, nothing, dirt. And I started to believe that. I got into drugs, trying to deal with my emotions. When I was high and drunk it felt great, I forgot I had problems. But afterward, they were still there, and using made them worse.

Back then, I kept trying to deny what was going on at my stepdad's. I felt like I lost myself. I lost who I was, what I stand for, who I am. I used to believe that the abuse was my fault. I thought if I wasn't female, a girl, it would not be happening to me. And I thought if other people knew, they would blame me and think that I'd asked for it.

For a while, I figured that if I got married that would take care of my problems. I would be on my own. I wouldn't have to worry about dealing with my stepdad. I slept with guys thinking that if they loved me they would marry me. But I had it backward. You have to respect yourself and love yourself first before you can have a relationship that works.

My stepdad was violent, too. I was afraid he'd come after me if I told. When he got mad at his new wife, he'd punch his fist through the wall. If he could do that, just imagine what he could do to me if I told my mom what he was doing to me.

It got so that every time we had to go over to his place, I felt like I wanted to kill myself. I was always scared something was going to happen. We'd be playing hide-and-seek with the little kids and he'd want to hide with me or my sister. It freaked me out.

One time we were over there for the night and his wife was gone. He told me his sexual fantasies about me and he wouldn't let me leave. He kept trying to take advantage of me and I kept trying to stop him. Finally, I went and slept with one of the younger kids so he'd leave me alone. I thought, "I really can't handle this. Maybe I should say something to my sister."

running away

It took a lot of strength for me to ask my sister. We hadn't ever talked about what my stepdad was doing. He is my sister's real father and I didn't want her mad at me. I was scared, too, because if it turned out I was the only one, people might think I was just trying to stir up trouble in the family. But I went ahead and asked.

When she told me, I was so glad I'd asked. When you find out there's another person it's happening to, it makes you both stronger. You can depend on each other to get it out in the open.

We talked in the backyard and decided to run away. We snuck out the back gate and ran down to the pay phone at the fast-food place a couple of blocks away. We called home collect and asked our mom's husband, Michael, to come get us. He sent my aunt out. Michael said he would have killed my stepdad if he'd seen him. That was the last thing that we needed. I'm glad he sent my aunt.

Michael called my stepdad and confronted him on the phone. My stepdad said that he'd done it and that he would call the cops on himself. And he did. He told them it had been going on for years. Maybe he wanted it to stop, too.

When my aunt came to get us, she was so in shock she couldn't say anything—and she usually talks a lot. She took us back to my stepdad's house to pack up our stuff. The cops were there. They questioned us and then said we could go home. They ended up arresting my stepdad that day.

When we got home, my mom acted like it wasn't really happening. I felt really bad for her. I think she wanted to be supportive but she didn't know how. And she must have been in shock—she'd been sending us kids over there for years. So in those first couple of days I talked with my aunt and my close friend and my grandma. Michael wanted to talk with me, too. At first it felt weird, him being a man and all, but it turned out that he was really helpful. It felt good knowing he was there for me, too.

A few days later I overheard my mom talking with her best friend about what had happened. That must have helped her because a little after that, she apologized and started crying. She said, "If I'd known about it, I would have stopped it. It would have stopped a long time ago."

After they arrested my stepdad, the cops made an appointment for me and my sister to go see a counselor at Children's Services. There, we were told that we would both be interviewed at the CAST office to give evidence about what my stepdad did to us. CAST stands for Child Abuse Services Team.

video evidence

I was nervous about the interview. I didn't know what they expected of me. I thought the lady who interviewed me would be totally up-tight. But she wore jeans and a nice shirt and I felt comfortable talking with her. I was relieved that she was a regular person like me or you.

She took me into a room that had big, soft couches. She told me that I could say what I wanted to say and that if I didn't feel like talking about something, I didn't have to. She didn't try to hide anything from me. She showed me that the room had a one-way mirror and told me that there were people behind it from the police and the district attorney's office. She told me that the interview would be video-taped and that it would be used as evidence.

Then she asked me questions and I answered them. I was glad she videotaped it because it saved me from having all those people question me separately. They had what they needed on the videotape. It took about half an hour. Then my sister went in after me. When it was over, I felt like a weight had been lifted from my shoulders.

My stepdad ended up plea bargaining. He was sentenced to sixteen years in prison. When he's out he has to register as a sex offender.

When he gets out, I'll be in my thirties. I want to face him and ask him why he did it. I want to know what he was thinking. It's important to me.

I don't understand why a grown man would want to do the things he did. It's disturbing. It's sick. He must have something wrong with him emotionally. I wonder if something bad happened to him when he was younger. My real father walked out on my life when I was really young and *his* father had walked out on him. Maybe what happened with my stepdad was part of a chain reaction, too. Or it could have been a power trip, you know, like he thought he was so manly because he could control a little girl.

The abuse had a major effect on my life. It made me feel like I was nobody, nothing. Like I didn't deserve to be here, I didn't deserve to breathe. I have to remind myself that it was not my fault. It's nice to hear it sometimes from other people, too. You can hear it, but it takes time to sink in. It helps me to remember that he is a grown man. I didn't have power over him. I blamed myself for not stopping him, but it's hard to control an adult, especially when you're a kid.

I have to remind myself that there are people who love me. My grandma, my mom, and Michael really care about me. It took me a while to realize I can respect myself, too. Once you start respecting yourself, people start treating you better.

Another long-term effect is that I have a hard time trusting guys. I'm afraid to be alone with them. I worry that something bad is going to happen. It's going to take me a while to get over that.

One guy told me, "It's in the past. Just forget it." You can't forget something like that, but you can work through it.

It helps that he was sent to jail. I feel like he got what he deserved. The cops and the people at CAST suggested that I get counseling. Counseling does help, but it was hard to find someone I could trust.

I didn't feel comfortable with the first three counselors I saw. They wanted copies of my journals and things like that. I thought, "What's up with that? That's not right!" Now I am seeing this really cool counselor. She's very down-to-earth and I can talk with her about anything. I really trust her.

That's something people don't realize when they go to counseling. Just because you run into one or two you don't like, it doesn't mean you should give up. Eventually you will find someone you can trust and you'll have a good relationship with them. Yeah, my counselor is paid to listen to my problems. But it's more than that. She's someone I can talk to who really wants to listen. She's like one of my really good friends. She actually cares.

She helps me with my self-esteem, helps me feel better when I'm feeling depressed about life or about the things that happened to me. She also helps me figure out my feelings. Sometimes it's hard for me to tell what my emotions are because of everything that happened to me. She helps with other things, too, boys and life and how to better myself.

For a while I went to group counseling. There were five other girls in my self-esteem group. They'd been through some of the same things I had. When the abuse was going on, I thought I was the only person in the world these things happened to and that I was to blame. It's funny, but when I heard what happened to the others, it was easier to see how it wasn't *their* fault.

The first counselor I went to figured out that I'm manic-depressive. It sucks to be bipolar. I want to be normal.

It's much better now that I'm on medication. It keeps me regular, having regular emotions, instead of crying one minute, happy the next, angry the next. I try to remember to take my medication because I don't like the effect when I'm off it.

Writing my thoughts down helps me, too. I have two journals. One with roses on it where I write down my feelings about my dad and my stepdad. In the other one I write about my friends and my boyfriends or when I'm upset at my parents, daily stuff like that. I write things down that I cannot tell other people.

What's so cool about keeping a journal is I can go back and read things and see how far I've come. When I read something four or five months later I see the changes in myself and realize I'm a different person now.

God is an important part of my life. When I don't have anybody to sit and talk with, when I feel alone, God is right there next to me. He carries me through the hardest times.

I have a favorite place I go to, too. I hike out on the cliffs and watch the ocean, feel how beautiful it all is. I feel like the waves can wash away my depression. Like I'm free, that nothing can hurt me. Just thinking about that place brings joy to me. When I'm depressed, I close my eyes and imagine the smell, the way it looks, the sounds. I feel like I could fly.

independence

After the abuse came out, I still lived with my mom and Michael. Recently, the three of us started to fight. I don't know why. It's really

stressful when you argue a lot. Then my school counselor told me about Launchpad.

Launchpad is supportive housing, an independent-living program where you learn to live on your own. I went and had an interview and got accepted and moved in. I share an apartment with two guys and they are slobs! The staff are like counselors; they are there to help us with things. We have to sign out, tell them where we're going, and be back by curfew. We have fake checking accounts so we can learn to balance a checkbook, make deposits, pay bills, and everything like that. They give us money to do grocery shopping and budgeting. We each have to cook three or four meals a week. It's really awesome.

Now that I'm out of the house, my mom and Michael and I have a really close relationship. My mom and I talk with each other and depend on each other—without arguing and fighting.

I'm happy now. I like where I'm living. My relationship with my parents is going great. I have a job I like and my own car.

Even school's going good. I'm dyslexic and have a hard time reading. One of my teachers in grade school told me that I was dumb and I wasn't going to amount to anything. But I got into special-ed classes and I've made it a long way since then. I'm getting good grades and I'll graduate from high school this June.

It's great to be eighteen. You get a little bit of freedom, you feel responsible. But it's also kind of scary at the same time. You're planning your whole life. When you get out there it's not as easy as you think it's going to be. You have to earn enough money to live on. Expenses are crazy!

inspiration

I work in a nursing home, helping the elderly. Right now I work in the activities part. I play games, talk with the clients, and help with Happy Hour. It's so much fun to just sit with them and play bingo and draw and make penny banks, things like that. They like to make snicker doodles; that's a cookie rolled in brown sugar. I'm thinking about taking the Certified Nursing Assistant class now so I can take vital signs and change and bathe them. I like to give to others, like working with the elderly, because it makes me feel better about myself.

After I graduate from high school, I'm going straight to junior college. I want to become a surgical nurse, but it is going to take years of schooling, so I'm going to take it in steps. First I'll get my RN at junior college and then transfer to state college.

My great-grandma is my inspiration. Anytime someone told her, "You can't do this," she did it. She was a mechanic and a truck driver. She drove buses and rode motorcycles and became a surgical nurse. She was a really cool lady. My grandma told me stories about her and ever since then I've wanted to become a surgical nurse.

I want to get married and have children, too. But I want to make sure I'm ready for them, that I have my job together and my life together and that I have the right guy. Make sure he's not going to do something stupid like disown his kids or molest them. He needs to be someone I can trust.

There are people who tell me I don't know anything about life. "You're too young to understand what life is about. Nothing bad happens to people your age." It's not true. They would be surprised what people my age go through. But what doesn't kill you makes you stronger. After everything comes out and you deal with it, you become a healthier person. You can go out and help other people who have been through the same situation. Or you can go and give the world whatever it is you want to give.

Arturo

Two key events shaped my life. One was my father's death. When I was eight he died in a fire. The other was this thing that happened with these two older guys when I was ten.

There were long periods of my life when I just put all of it on the shelf and said, "I'm not going to worry about this stuff." I shut it out. I didn't talk about it to anybody, not until I was twenty-one and faced some tough choices. And then recently it all came up again.

the fire

Growing up, we had a normal life. At least that's how I saw it at the time. I have a brother two years older than me and three sisters. We were raised in San Francisco in the Mission District, with only my immediate family and one uncle. Everybody else was back in Mexico.

My mother had a job in a warehouse. She was tough, strong, and hardworking. My dad was like a little god to me, I looked up to him so much. I never saw him work, but every night he and his friends had a mariachi band at the house. They played full-blown mariachi music, without the uniforms but with the big bass *guitarras* and the little *requintos* and trumpets and everything else. They played for themselves. They would just party down.

One night, my brother woke me up. I couldn't breathe because there was so much smoke pouring into the dining room where we slept. My brother tried to open the door because we could hear someone screaming on the other side.

Right when I was passing out, a window broke and a fireman came through. I woke up in the hospital and my mother came in all bandaged up. I asked her where my father was and she told me he was in a room down the hall. Later on, in the hospital chapel, she told me and my brother that our father died in the fire. The scream I had heard was my father dying. From that moment on, I changed.

I became angry and withdrawn. I was really hurt that my mom lied to me. It wasn't fair to blame my mother, but I did. I blamed Mexico. I blamed God. I blamed everybody.

After the fire, I was so sick from the smoke that I could hardly breathe. I don't remember much during that period, it was like a big fog, but I do remember I flunked third grade.

When my father died, everything in my family changed, too. My mother worked two jobs to keep us in parochial school. We were left alone a lot. My brother was only ten years old and all of a sudden he had to take over, be like our parent. Our uncle who lived with us was from the old school and he used a whip to discipline us. The bottom line was that my brother and I didn't have the father that we needed.

seduced

I started hanging out on the streets. My neighborhood was multicultural. Black guys, white guys, Latino guys, we were all good friends.

On the street we started dibbling and dabbling with alcohol. We ran pretty wild.

When I was ten these two grownups would hang out with us and play outdoor sports like stickball, yard games. They seemed like nice guys. They used to take me with them to this place, an apartment across town, where they had all these indoor games. They hugged me; there was a lot of warmth. When I was with them, I felt good about myself. Someone was loving me and caring about me. I thought it was okay.

Looking back, I should have been more open about what I was up to with these guys all along, not kept secrets from my mom. But they said, "Don't tell anybody," and it was fun.

At that point they were just nice guys who loved me. There was a lot of cuddling and caressing. In my family, we didn't hug that way. Not this body-to-body stuff. But I figured that's just how these guys showed themselves toward me. I remember really clearly that I trusted them. At that point, it all felt good.

Then it started to progress. It went to two of us lying on the bed, hugging, rubbing against each other. Always with clothes on. One time with one guy, one time with the other. Then, the last time, they were both there.

What they did was, well, they held me down, they stripped me, and they raped me.

It hurt like hell.

I was only ten. I didn't understand what was going on. I freaked out. Afterward, I went into the kitchen and got a knife. I came back and stuck one of those guys in the butt. Then I ran. It was the last time I ever saw them.

I ran and I ran. I tried to find my way home. It was all the way across town and I got lost on the way, but eventually I made it.

I never forgot what those two guys did, but I didn't tell anyone either. I never told my mother because I thought she would have been completely devastated and I was afraid I'd be in trouble.

I didn't understand why it happened. Here I was with these guys and they seemed so nice and then all of a sudden they did this to me. I couldn't figure it out. And I felt so bad inside. I didn't realize there was this emotion called shame, and that's what I was feeling—ashamed, embarrassed, humiliated.

After that, I started really running the streets. I felt even more anger, more hostility than before. My friends and I started smoking dope. Then one of them introduced me to sniffing glue. We just ran amuck.

Out at Golden Gate, Dolores, and Aquatic parks, there was a lot of drumming going on. There would be twenty to thirty *congueros* out playing Afro-Cuban rhythms. I was one of those kids who always wanted to know "Why do you do this?" "How do you play that?" "Why do you do this slap?" "What's that tone?" I used to drive the drummers crazy because I was so intrigued by the drumming. So one guy, this great guy, put me at the end of the bench, got someone to pull out a drum for me, and gave me a pattern to learn. That was the beginning of my drumming career.

It was great because I was involved in something that I loved and it was a lot of fun. Some good musicians came out of that scene. Carlos Santana was just this crazy kid up the street who played his guitar all the time. The problem for me was that I was so into drugs I didn't practice. You've got to practice a lot to make it as a professional musician.

I was fourteen when I first stuck a needle in my arm. I was running with a couple of guys from my street who were shooting speed. They were further into drugs than me and I was the kid they always wanted to shake off. I was a wannabe.

Even though I was into drugs, I liked high school at first. I passed ninth grade with no problem. All this time, I still had a lot of anger. I was so withdrawn, I wouldn't talk about it. It built up into this hostility that I always had inside me. Then, in tenth grade, I punched out a teacher at school. I just didn't want to go to school anymore. That did devastate my mother.

heroin

By sixteen I was knee-deep in heroin. Heroin is a great reliever of pain. I used it to block out the emotional pain from what I went through—my father dying, me being so sick from the fire, the molestation, the rape. I never talked with anybody about my feelings. I didn't know that I needed to. Instead, trying to block it all out, I got addicted to heroin.

Once you're addicted, it's not just a matter of choosing to get high. The drug takes over. The biggest thing is not wanting to get sick, which is what happens when you can't get more of your drug and you start going through withdrawal. So you lead a life of crime to get money to get the drugs to stop feeling sick. All you care about is one thing—how am I going to get my hustle today? It's about survival.

And when it's about survival, you don't feel guilt, shame, or remorse. That comes later.

We used to hustle pharmaceuticals. Me and my buddies would burglarize pharmacies to get these pills. Then we made our rounds to the different high schools, selling to other kids.

When I was eighteen I got this gal pregnant. I was told that if I didn't marry her I would never see my child, so we had a shotgun wedding. I wanted to be a good dad. During the whole pregnancy I stopped using. I got a job working as a tank cleaner for the government, making good money.

Then, the night that my son was born, my partners and I were drinking beer out front of my mom's place. We started smoking dope. Somebody pulled out some heroin and *boom!* off I went. Once I started using again, I couldn't stop.

From eighteen to twenty-one years old I went kind of crazy. I don't know how many times I overdosed. I was in and out of jail and trying to keep my marriage going. But I couldn't stop using heroin. What was so tragic was that I was repeating a lot of what my father did in the past and I didn't even know it. I mean the lifestyle with drugs and alcohol. And I was violent. If my wife looked at someone else, I would slap her. My mom told me not to treat my wife the way my dad had treated her.

Some of the things I've done in my life I don't feel good about.

the choice

Things got worse before they got better. My wife had enough; she left me for good. I was twenty-one years old and had something like thirty arrests.

At twenty-one I got convicted of possession of heroin and possession of stolen property. They were going to send me to the state penitentiary for two two-to-tens running wild, which means two consecutive sentences. That's four to twenty years in prison.

But I was really lucky. I had a lawyer from Mission Legal Defense, a group of lawyers who helped impoverished people. He worked it out so I had a choice—go to the joint or go into a residential drug treatment program.

I chose rehabilitation. At first, they wanted to send me to a place for hard-core addicts and criminals. But deep inside, despite everything I'd done, I felt that wasn't me. My lawyer found a place for me at Walden House, and that's where I went, straight from county jail. The deal was I had to go through the program and stay clean for five years or go back to jail.

Walden House is a twenty-four-hour live-in therapeutic community. Back then, it was in this big beautiful Victorian home. There was group therapy, one-on-one counseling, and family therapy. The residents themselves ran a lot of the program. We worked on the service crew, answered the phone, drove vehicles, and cooked. It was all a learning process.

It's called rehabilitation, but some of us didn't have the skills to begin with, so it was more like habilitation. In essence, I grew up there.

We went through a series of group meetings where we talked about our issues. A lot of the people in the program were white kids from the suburbs and I was Latin, a little *cholo* punk wannabe. At first, I didn't trust anybody. But in the groups, people talked freely; they could just be themselves and it was okay. And I found out that other people had gone through much worse than me. No matter what had happened to you—heroin, speed, being molested or raped, committing crimes, being a crime victim—someone in the group could relate to it. No matter what, it was okay to talk about it, to say how you felt. You could try to figure out some of the things that had happened to you and what you really wanted for your life.

Also, I had a couple of great counselors. There were times when I didn't want to talk about stuff in full group, but I could turn to my counselor and say, "Hey, I'm going crazy with these thoughts. Am I really out of whack?" I worked through a lot, talking about the things that affected me. It helped me get off drugs. I completed the program in fourteen months. Thank you, Walden House!

phobia

There was this one guy who was my counselor for eight months. He was the straightest-looking guy, like a businessman, very professional, very articulate. He did my body search when I came into the program. I respected this man so much because of who he was and how he treated me. A couple of months later, I realized that he was gay.

It freaked me out because I trusted him. I had told him a lot of my stuff about what happened. I couldn't believe that somebody I entrusted with my life turned out to be one of "those people"! Well, I had this phobia. I was homophobic. I ended up working through that with him, but it was a hard transition.

You know, I could have gone on hating any man who would look at another male—man or boy—that way. But as far as I'm concerned, two consenting adults can do what they want. Acting sexual with a person who is not of legal age is a whole other matter. It's wrong.

It's too easy for an adult to manipulate a kid into what the adult wants to do—for the adult's satisfaction. A child or teenager is going to believe that they are in a safe place, with a friend. To betray that trust is wrong, people get hurt. There are good reasons why it's against the law.

After I got out of the program, a friend and I shared an apartment. I got a job recapping tires. The people at Walden House were like my family. I'd stop by, stay in touch. One day the clinical director offered me a job. I was twenty-three with all this insane energy. He was a little concerned about whether I could stay focused enough. But I was so honored, I told him, "If you hire me, I will become a career employee and I will be one of your best employees."

And I did. I was. I worked my way up to vice president in charge of operations.

fatherhood

I married again and had a second son. Now I'm an active father to them both. My kids are great, but raising kids is a tough job.

I don't hit. That lifestyle has been behind me for many, many years. I would never go back to that. I remember being yelled at, too. I made a conscious decision at a young age that I wouldn't do the same thing to my kids.

You have to look at things not just from the parent's point of view, but remember what it was like being a kid and look through those eyes, too. Remembering that helps me. Sometimes I'm frustrated and sometimes I'm loud. But that fear that the child goes through hearing that screeching voice is so fresh in my heart, I wouldn't wish that on anybody. I try to treat my kids good.

relapse

If I stopped right here, the story would be "This guy got himself into recovery and got his life together." But that's not the whole story. The reality is if you don't take care of yourself and keep your life in balance, you can lose yourself.

For a while, working for the program, I drank excessively, but I never really acknowledged it. And for a long time, the stuff from my childhood lay dormant inside me. What I didn't realize was how it contributed to my drinking. Bottom line is I checked myself into residential treatment a second time. Fortunately Walden House was in total support of me going out on leave and getting my act together. When I came back I had to work up through the ranks again.

What I learned is that some people can drink socially, have half a glass of wine and that's it. I'm not one of them. I know that for a fact now. Addiction is about avoiding what's inside you, avoiding doing what you need to do to be at peace with yourself. I hadn't felt good about being me. That was part of the growing that I still had to do. I had to develop the emotional muscle to build a life for myself without relying on drugs *or* alcohol.

I had to go through more counseling to work through the sexual abuse at a deeper level, to try to understand it and then let go of it. Sometimes the rage is still there, inside me. I let it out as I need to and I try to do it in a way that won't hurt people.

Now I go to Alcoholics Anonymous as well as 12-step meetings for drug abuse. I do it religiously. I work the steps, I have a sponsor. That's really important for anyone who has followed the path of substance abuse. Not everyone needs residential treatment, but you need to have a program and stick to it.

the music world

I learned to find a balance between work, play, family life, quiet time—the spiritual side. By spiritual I don't mean finding God, because for me it's not about religion, although I did join some folks who do Buddhist chanting.

Music really helps me spiritually. I've played in bands all along, but now I give it more time. I'm in two bands. In my brother's we play Tex-Mex, Tejano, Cumbia, Norteño—all that traditional Latino music. And the other—do you know what *soka* is? It's this insane music from the islands of Trinidad and Tobago. We play concerts, parties, clubs.

The music world has a lot of substance partying, but the trend today is that it's okay not to drink, not to use. You can still have a good time. When we go somewhere to play, the guys in the band say, "This one don't drink, put some coffee on for him." It's a good support system. Some of them drink socially, nobody smokes *ganja* or chases anything. The guys know who can do what and are respectful of that. They are very, very good people.

There is something else I want to say. Even though I haven't stuck a needle in my arm in twenty-five years, being an IV drug user, sharing needles, I exposed myself to hepatitis C. This last year I had myself

checked and I've got inflammation of the liver. It put a shock wave through me.

Now I have a responsibility not only to myself but to my kids to live the best possible life I can, for the longest amount of time I can. And it's true, you need to take each day like it is your last. Enjoy it as much as you possibly can. That's important. Nobody can promise you tomorrow.

Tino

THANKS FOR DOING THIS INTERVIEW HERE, out of doors. As a kid I spent a lot of time playing in this creek, building dams, chasing water skeeters. This park was a sanctuary for me, a place where I could get away from my grandmother and the stress of our household, a place where my exuberance wasn't a problem, where I could be me. It's probably one of the few places where I felt safe, where I felt nurtured and nourished.

For most of the first five years of my life we lived with my grandmother. My parents were having problems and my dad lived in another state. When we lived with my grandmother, I was repeatedly molested by her.

conflict

She would molest me when we were alone together, usually in her room or when she gave me a bath. This isn't easy to say out loud—what she did was masturbate me and she forced me to nurse on her breast.

My grandmother was a great manipulator. When I was with her, there was always my favorite candy or my favorite television show. Whenever my mom and I argued, my grandmother would side with me. There was all this adoration. "Tino's such a beautiful child." It felt good. I look back on it now and see it was a setup.

The incest ended when I was five. I was on my grandmother's lap, on the couch in her living room. She used to wear pins, brooches, on her dress. She had me sucking at her breast and my mom came into the room. My grandmother pulled or jerked my head away and my cheek got cut on her brooch. I was crying. My grandmother's dress was open to her waist and she had her bra undone. She said something to my mother that I didn't understand and that was it. She stopped. That was the end of the abuse.

That summer my dad came back into the picture and we moved to

Boston. I was so happy to be living with my dad and away from my grandmother. I didn't forget what had happened, but I pushed it way back in my mind and shut the door. I didn't want to think about it. I had a new life ahead of me.

We lived near the Fenway and I spent a lot of time in the park. I climbed trees. In the winter I ice-skated on the creek. I did a lot of art and spent time in museums, too. When I was about twelve we moved back here, to my grandmother's neighborhood.

Shortly after puberty, I started feeling a lot of internal conflict and confusion regarding my sexuality. If anything sexual came up, I went into a state of dissociation and fear. I felt damaged, unworthy. I felt that if I was in a relationship with a girl it would turn out to be very damaging for her, for me. So I had this dance. There was a lot of attraction and chasing—I longed for a girlfriend—but I would shy away before things got past holding hands.

By the time I was fifteen, I started drinking, mostly beer. This is a college town and it was pretty easy for high school kids to sneak into fraternity parties. By the time I was seventeen, I was drinking hard stuff on a regular basis. I became sort of a drunken party fool. By being loud and obnoxious I was trying to be a big person. Inside, I felt like a scared little boy.

control

It was important for my family that I go to college. I chose to major in forestry—primarily, I can see in retrospect, to avoid contact with people. In forestry, I could be nurturing without having to deal with the emotions that come with human relationships. Also, it was a way for me to get back to nature, to the place where I'd felt safe as a child.

Finances dictated that I live at home. My grandmother was living only a block away. There was always an undercurrent of tension between the two of us when she was in the house, and she was in the house pretty much every day. In a sense, I was prostituting myself; I can't think of a softer way to say it. Part of the financing of my education came from her. I didn't accuse or confront her, knowing that I was having part of what I wanted paid for. But there was a real deep-seated anger that I kept under the surface.

By the time I was twenty-two, it was really apparent to me where I was headed with alcohol. Something inside me snapped and I realized, "Ain't no way! This is not the road I want to travel on!"

So I quit drinking, but I began to starve myself. I limited myself to 800 to 1,000 calories daily and exercised two or three times a day. I went from weighing about 165 pounds right when I quit drinking to 120. I wasn't healthy, I was fanatical.

Alcohol abuse and anorexia really did serve a purpose. They kept my emotions quiet. They kept a lid on the anger and the molest memories for several years. When I quit doing the addictions, I let all the scary lions and tigers out.

At first it felt very empowering. I could shout down anybody. I became very controlling of others, verbally abusive. At work, I would bully people around. When I blew up, I felt powerful, self-righteous. But afterward I felt ashamed and scared.

the dream

Then my grandmother died. I went to see her in the hospital out of a sense of obligation. It was her third recurrence of cancer and she was on megadoses of morphine. My sister was in the room, but she dozed off, so I was the only one to witness my grandmother's passing. It spooked me. Just the passing of life, being mortal, was shocking enough. All the tension in her body, all the pain, just left with her. That was powerful to witness.

I felt such sadness. Sorrow for her condition and sadness that there wasn't going to be an opportunity to express to her the pain, the shame, that came from the molest. We couldn't resolve it face-to-face anymore. That opportunity was gone.

A few months later, I woke up one night in sheer terror, bolt upright in bed, drenched in sweat, screaming "NO!"

My grandmother had walked with a cane. She always stirred up trouble with her walking stick. In the dream, she was approaching me with that stick and poking at me with it and I just grabbed it and broke it over my knee and threw it back at her. I was yelling "NO!" at her when I woke up.

That dream startled the hell out of me. At the same time, I was having relationship problems and a legal battle with a neighbor. I felt like I was out there and alone. The stress of it all just got to me. I thought I was having a mental breakdown. I mean, I was. It was suicide or call the hotline.

1-800-suicide

At that point I felt like it might be better to commit suicide than to pick up the phone and admit to somebody "I have a problem. I'm having mental confusion, stress that I can't control." Admitting that there were things I couldn't control was so frightening that I almost would have rather taken my own life.

But I called—in a tearful voice, quivering, barely able to verbalize what was going on. The person on the other end asked some pertinent questions, like, was I thinking about causing harm to myself or others? I probably lied a little bit and minimized it and said no, I wasn't. Just hearing that voice on the other end of the phone line calmed me down quite a bit. I'm surprised at how reassuring hearing that voice was. No judgments at all, just "Tell me where you're at. Tell me what's going on."

They referred me to a local psychotherapist and I went. But I didn't continue after the first eight months. All I wanted to talk about was the legal hassle with my neighbor. The therapist basically said, "Until you're ready to talk about the things that are causing you to be so angry and feel such anguish, we're not going to get anywhere."

breakthrough

So there was another year of nightmares and flashbacks. The kicker happened when I was in an antique shop. Someone brought in a picture that had the exact same detail as the wallpaper that was in my grandmother's room. It was an idyllic scene, this country farm with tilled hillsides and apple trees and a guy driving a tractor.

When I saw it, instantaneous reaction. I almost threw up right there on the spot.

Feelings of panic and terror flooded me. Those were feelings I'd had as a little child. Hopeless and helpless. I didn't know what the heck was going to come next. I was also getting strange body sensations. I felt like I was going to vomit, to purge myself. Total tension and terror in my pelvic area. I just wanted to curl up in bed with the covers over my head. I didn't want anyone to see me. I had kept the door to my grandmother's room shut in my mind and all of a sudden here's this little piece of wallpaper and everything falls out.

This time I didn't call the hotline, though I was probably having a classic mental breakdown—or breakthrough, as I have come to see it. Now I knew I needed help and that I needed to focus on the incest in therapy.

I didn't go to just any therapist. I called a friend who was a molest survivor and asked if she could recommend someone. I felt comfort knowing that my friend trusted him. I was a little bit nervous sitting in the waiting room because the guy was local—there was a very good chance that somebody I knew might see me there. But at that point, I knew I couldn't let that stop me.

I interviewed him and he interviewed me. He honestly told me, straight up front, "I'm not sure how far I'm going to be able to go with you on this, but if you are willing to try, then I'm willing to try." I felt an affinity, a trust, from that moment on.

It felt really good to finally be able to tell my story, to have someone acknowledge and validate what I was going through. To tell me that I wasn't crazy, that I wasn't weird, that this was a normal reaction to what my grandmother did.

When the therapist first introduced the term PTSD, post-traumatic stress disorder, I thought, "What's this got to do with me?" Then he showed me a video clip of a guy who'd had to sever his own arm to get out from underneath a tree that had fallen on him. To see this blank stare on the guy's face and to hear his monotone voice recounting the story, it just clicked. That could just as easily have been me saying "Yes, I was abused by my grandmother and it happened early in my childhood but I really don't remember all that much so I don't think it is very important to go there."

It became very clear that this therapist was with me the whole way. I could say what was for me the most painful, the most vile, the most hurtful thing that had happened to me and he didn't shy away. He witnessed the whole thing.

During my time in therapy I attended a men's support group. It was not a molest survivor group. This was just men getting together dealing with the issues in their lives. Surprisingly, many of the men had been sexually abused in childhood, but I was the only one who wanted to go deeper with the issue. Everybody else said things like "Yep, that is what happened, but the real issue is how I am relating

to my girlfriend. The real issue is I don't get along with my boss at work. The real issue . . ." But we did get into making masks and I chose to work on images that came to me in dreams.

When I make a mask, when I wear it, it feels like I'm bringing forth a part of me that already exists, I'm giving it voice. This eagle mask came from a very powerful dream. It's a metaphor for my creative self, my true self.

For some people drugs like Prozac might be right. For me, creative expression is how I manage, how I deal with strong emotions. I don't try to negate them, I don't try to diminish them, I don't try to observe them from afar. And I don't try to numb them out—I know where that leads from my experience with alcohol.

Through dreams, poetry, mask making, I work with metaphor. Metaphor for me means getting a very condensed picture to express a bigger thing. Sometimes I still can't find the words for my feelings, but I can express them artistically, so I don't keep them bottled up.

love and sex

The most important part of healing was reclaiming my sexuality. I used to feel contaminated, damaged. Because I felt I would be a danger to others, I repressed my sexual feelings. A lot of it was wanting sexual gratification but not wanting touch. I *did not* want touch, even if it was gentle touch. I felt like that was just a way to entice me into the actual abuse that was going to happen later.

I didn't become sexually active until I felt the desperation of turning twenty-one and I thought, "My God, I'm still a virgin. It would be horrible if anybody finds out!" In actuality, it was pretty damaging to rush into something like that in an unconscious way. I wasn't respectful to myself or to the young woman. I carried a lot of shame about it. Recently she and I talked about it. I apologized to her and she was very understanding. That was good for both of us.

How did I reclaim my sexuality? By being in a relationship with somebody who is open, direct, and honest. I've never been more in love with another person than I am with my wife, Karla.

With us there's no pressure or forced intimacy. We don't push for sex if the other person's not interested. And if feelings come up that are related to the past, we stop and talk about them. I can say, "I'm feeling afraid because when you touch me that way it reminds me of another piece of the molest." We comfort and console each other. Because we can go to those painful places, we can also go to more joyful ones. It's a stronger bond, being compassionate with each other.

And then, when we do connect sexually, there's all that trust. I'm not afraid of being hurt or hurting her. I feel completely safe. Now sex is nurturing. It's a deep connection with someone else that is based on mutual respect. It's a spiritual experience.

confronting God

Spirituality is something else I had to reclaim from my grandmother. She was a follower of Meher Baba, of Krishnamurti, all these peaceful, loving people. Because of this association with her, I had a distaste for anything spiritual. There were actually a lot of really interesting things about this lady. I had to blow them up, burn them up, throw them out of my life, in order to get to the place where I can look back and say, "Wow, you know, that's pretty cool."

There's this Irish saying, "If you love God, you'll know Him in twenty years; if you hate Him, you'll know Him in two." With Karla's encouragement, I was willing to be pissed at God and to ask the question "Why was I abused?"

Before, I didn't want to hear the answer. I thought it was going to be "Because you were bad." I've come to find that that is not the way it is, at least not for me. I don't carry that belief or that resentment anymore. Karla helped me see that I always had a connection with spirit and that it was unique and individual.

I feel a very strong spiritual connection to the earth. These trees here, this creek, they protected me, they nurtured me, they helped me get through a real tough time. There is this whole, underlying, unseen network of animals and plants—and people, too—that provide all of this support to us every day.

Was healing worth it? Yeah. Completely. Totally. I've got to say that it is not an easy path. My capacity to feel and attain joy was completely linked with my capacity to feel pain. They are totally tied to each other. As I became aware of my own feelings, I became aware of the feelings of others. And I found a tremendous depth of compassion and empathy that I never would have touched before.

Odd as it may seem, I bless my grandmother today. I'm not talking about that "forgive and forget" b.s. that people use when they want you to shut down emotionally because what you went through is too painful for *them* to hear about. To heal, I needed to go through all the emotions that I had no way to deal with as a small child. But now I've come to a place where there's closure.

I know that my grandmother was more than just the molest. She could also be a very generous and kind and loving person. I certainly suspect that there were childhood traumas that she was acting out on me. Now I think of her with compassion.

Sexual assault—child abuse—is horrific. It should never happen to anybody. But healing from this wound has given me tremendous gifts. If I hadn't been through these experiences, I wouldn't be the person I am today.

Akaya

MY FATHER WASN'T BORN AN ABUSER. He was born a squirmy, warm, brown-skinned boy. He was just a little bundle of possibility that his mama held in her arms and wished the best for. I know that. And then some atrocious thing happened to him. When terrible things get done to people, they can get twisted up inside.

mother's love

This may sound strange in light of what happened in my family, but there was never a moment in my life when I did not *know* that I was deeply loved by at least one other person. And that has made all the difference.

It started with my mother, who loved me. I never doubted her love, ever. So there was a part of me that was always healthy. It's the part of me that assumes that in any given situation and at any given time, I will be loved, accepted, and wanted.

She'd grown up very poor and she was determined never, ever to be poor again. She made choices about her own life and the lives of her children based on that. My dad was in the military, so his was a steady income. She worked, too, as a secretary. I think she would say poverty was the greatest horror she could ever imagine and she was not going to raise her kids in it. Now, I would say that abuse is the greatest horror that I can imagine. I would rather raise my kids in poverty than in abuse. But I don't know poverty.

My father grew up during the Depression, one of six children in a very, very poor family and with a violent father who beat the kids unmercifully. My father was the best and brightest of his peer group; he learned to speak French, he was his high school valedictorian. He escaped from home as soon as he could by joining the military, but he did not forget his father's physical violence. He and my mother made a deep commitment to never hit their kids.

My parents were unusual people for their time. As soon as it became illegal to discriminate in terms of housing, we moved into a white community. Two weeks after we moved in, someone burned a cross on our lawn. That was a scary time, but my parents stayed on. They also chose not to raise us in a church. Until I was in ninth grade, I was the only black student in my class. My younger sister and I grew up with good schools but without the support of a strong black community around us.

at home

My father was an alcoholic. As soon as he got home from work, he started to drink. He would lie on the couch, drunk or asleep. We operated around him. It felt like he didn't really exist in our household except when he'd get up and we'd feed him. And he mowed the lawn.

I don't think I saw him express any affection toward my mother in all the time they were married. I don't remember ever having heard him say "I love you" to me, my sister, or my mother. He didn't seem to *connect* with anybody—the abuse might have been the only way he knew how. I think somewhere inside he had become a very distorted, twisted human being who needed to be close to someone and had no way to do that except through force.

The abuse started when I was about two and stopped for a while when I was seven. I cried out one night when he was molesting me. My mother came into the room and he left. She stayed in my bed with me for the rest of the night. When I hit puberty and started to mature, my father started molesting me again. It was like he couldn't keep his hands off.

He made me participate. That was one of the hardest things to deal with later on, when I was healing. There were these verbal games he made me play. Like he would touch me and ask, "Whose breasts are these?" and I would have to tell him they were his. For me, at twelve, when this began, it registered that this was true, that he did own my breasts.

going to the stars

How I coped was I learned to split—to completely dissociate my mind from what was happening to my body. He'd walk into the room and I would disappear. I called it "going to the stars."

It was like there was a tunnel that I could climb into and I would be somewhere some-when else. I would be in the stars. He would do whatever he needed to do. Then, when it was over, my body would signal me that I could come back. Afterward, I didn't remember what he'd done. In some ways it was like it hadn't happened.

In splitting, what I did was preserve the core part of me—the essential, spiritual me. It was like protecting the seed of me so that when it was safe enough I could grow from there.

If I hadn't done that, I think I would have ended up in a mental institution. I know I might have killed myself.

escape

While all this was going on, in junior high and high school, I was among the best and brightest. I was really smart and gifted physically, too. I played varsity basketball and field hockey, went out for track and field. Senior class president, homecoming queen, valedictorian—

I don't think anybody could have done more than I did. All of it, I'm sure, was a way of escaping being at home.

During baseball season, I dated the captain of the football team and during football season I dated the captain of the baseball team—you had to have someone to go to the games with! And it wasn't like my sexual self was lost to me. I remembered all my first independent experiences, the boys I went out with, the kissing we did, the first attractions I felt to other girls. But anything that had to do with my father and sex together—somehow that got shelved on the other side of awareness. I had years of training in not remembering *that*.

Dissociation and hyperachievement were the ways I coped, but they couldn't stop the abuse. At home my life was hell. My father, wow, he had no boundaries whatsoever. The abuse happened several times a week. And it got more and more intense as I got older.

When I was a senior my father raped me really violently. I had been accepted to five different universities and I had a National Merit Scholarship, so it was clear that I was leaving home. But he decided that I wasn't going anywhere—that I was his. I was seventeen and he was determined to break me. He never did, because I could see my way out.

Oh, yes, I did go to college. I was so glad to get out of there! In that first semester, I came home for a visit. I was staying in my bedroom. My father came in and I told him, "No! I don't want to!" And he said, "As long as you are in my house, you will do what I tell you." That was the last time I ever went home until he moved out. As soon as my sister hit high school, my mom divorced him.

I went to college but dropped out in my junior year. I worked a lot of different jobs. It was a heady time for me. I was free and on my own, discovering myself as a young lesbian and as an African-American woman. I found my community, the people I chose to be with, the places where I felt at home.

Then my mother got sick. Before she died, I made her two promises. One was to finish my college education, and the other was to take her ashes to Jamaica, where she had hoped to retire. It took me a while, but I fulfilled both of my promises to her.

Then I moved to northern California to go to graduate school and stayed and got my consulting business started. One day I got a phone call from my father's neighbor. He'd taken my father to the emergency room. My father was drinking himself to death. The doctor said that he had less than a week to live unless something drastic happened.

My sister was living on the other side of the country, and had children and health problems of her own, so it was up to me. I went down and did the rescue thing. I transferred him to a hospital up here, packed all his stuff, got him stabilized.

My father went from the hospital into convalescent care and then to assisted living. He kept getting better and better because he wasn't drinking and they were feeding him. After I got him settled into a good place, got his finances organized, paid his bills, within two months of that, the memories came back.

When all that happened, I was thirty-six years old. I had taken on the executive director position of a nonprofit. My consulting business had taken off. I was sitting on a couple of national boards. My external life looked really, really extraordinary. Internally I was a mess.

Strange things started happening to my body. I would start to shake. I wanted to crawl under the table. And I had no idea what was going on. By then I had gone to graduate school in clinical psychology and I thought maybe this was late-onset schizophrenia. It took about two weeks of this kind of body stuff before an actual memory happened.

The memories came in pieces. At first it was smell. I could smell him. And then from the smell I could feel him. After the sense of touch came sight—I could see what happened. After I saw it, I could hear it and it became a whole piece.

As you can imagine, I was a wreck, just a wreck! I got into therapy as a result. I mean, I felt, "Oh, my God, what is going on?" I went into a serious depression.

Suddenly the foundation of my life was torn apart. I had built a story about my life that edited out major stuff so that I could survive. What I was remembering, and reexperiencing, was the history of the abuse in my life—a history I hadn't allowed myself to know.

Going to the stars as a child had saved me. It saved my sanity, maybe even my life. It held aside the part of me that I needed to have stay intact. It allowed me to endure years of abuse and to hold myself together afterward.

But now, what I had believed about myself turned out not to be true. The person I thought I was got torn up and thrown into the air and the pieces lay around with no connection. The work of healing was to take those pieces—plus these vivid, concrete memories of the abuse—and put them back together into a coherent picture.

I had great therapy. If I'd had a less skilled therapist, she might have labeled me with something like multiple personality disorder. But she didn't operate that way. She was like, "Okay, here's a human being who is really working hard to figure herself out and this is just how it is playing out." Her focus was on my wholeness all the way through.

phone sex

Early on in my healing, I decided to confront my father. I went to see him and told him that I was remembering incest.

He said, "Well, now, what is incest?" So I explained it to him. And he said, "Well, what do you remember exactly?" He kept asking for details, so I told him, chapter and verse. And he said, "I don't remember that."

Then, about two days later he called me and said, "Baby, what did you say happened between us?" And I said, "Incest." And he said, "Now, what is that again?" And we went through the whole thing, chapter and verse, again.

I was kind of slow on the uptake, but after the third call I got it. He was doing the same thing with me as before—only this time it was over the phone, it was phone sex. I thought to myself, "No way am I going to do this with him!"

I had to take care of myself. I had to protect that vulnerable part of myself that was just beginning to heal. So I told him I wasn't going to see him or talk with him anymore.

The decision to heal was a big decision, one I had to make almost daily. It was a commitment. "I will figure this out. I will heal from this. I will not put up with half a life. I will not!"

I don't want this to sound churchy, but I don't think I would have been able to remember if I hadn't had a spiritual foundation. Prior to awakening spiritually, I felt that this moment, this life, was all I could count on. The immensity of what I was about to remember wouldn't have had a large enough container.

When my mother died, that's when I began to awaken spiritually. I think Spirit—or God—was just kind of tapping her foot, going "I'm here, Akaya. Tell me when you decide to wake up." And finally I was ready and she said, "Okay, here we go!"

Sharon, my partner then, was learning all about women's spirituality and taught me. By the time I remembered the abuse, I'd had several years of conversations with Spirit and so I had enough of a foundation. I could literally rest some of the burden in the arms of the Mother. There were times when, if I hadn't had something larger than myself to rest in, I know I would not have made it.

And I understand that when I went to the stars as a child, I was being held in the Mind of God. I wouldn't have been able to describe it that way when it happened, but that's how I see it now.

Sharon was terrific. My healing was a journey for both of us. We really held each other's hands going through it. My friend Staci had done some healing herself and she kept telling me, "You can do this."

My sister never doubted what had happened. She said he'd tried the same thing with her when she was about ten, but she told him, "NO!" and he backed off. She stopped him! I was so glad for her and

113

proud of her, too. As I healed, my sister's support and her love for me made all the difference in the world.

reaching out

I knew it was time for me to talk with other survivors. I needed a support group. Since I couldn't find the group I wanted, I started one. I asked Staci, "Do you want to be part of this?" and she said yes. And another friend, Maria, said yes. And then another woman. You know, I had to find folks who were willing to laugh, to take it seriously, but not too seriously.

Earlier, when somebody told me, "One day you'll be able to laugh about this," I thought they were nuts. I said, "How can you laugh about this? This is *incest*!"

But, girl, have I laughed about incest! Laughter is great medicine. It's the antidote to despair. It's the place where I can remember that I am *not* incest. I am not sexual abuse, although it is a part of my history, any more than I am racism, although it's a part of my history, too.

Did I ever feel like a victim? Sure. Understanding what happened to me as a child is what helped me get sane. But I didn't want to stay in that place. I needed to move very quickly through victimhood.

There was a period of time when, if I wasn't at work, my focus was on the abuse or the healing of it. It took most of my energy. What told me that I was going to make it, that I had turned the corner, was when I started spending more time living than healing.

Then there came a moment when I realized it had been a month or so since I'd thought about the abuse. And I went, "Wow!" I'd known I was going to get there because I had gone through a time of grief when my mother died. Healing is a lot like grief. There is a hump in healing, too. As you are chugging up the hill and especially the last three or four yards, it doesn't look like you are ever going to get there, but you do. You get there.

confrontations

Six years after the memories came back, I decided to go see my father. I'd done buckets of therapy, been in my group, all of that. And all that time I'd been taking care of his finances, but I did not want to see him. Now I felt ready.

Staci went with me to the senior living home. He was a really old man, almost eighty. Age and alcohol abuse had taken their toll. He said, "Why haven't you come to see me?"

I said, "Do you remember the last time we talked? We talked about the sexual abuse between us. I needed to take some time away from you to deal with that and heal from it. And that's what I've done."

And he said, "I really don't remember those days. I believe you, but I don't remember."

I was really in a funk for a couple of days. I talked with my sister, wrote in my journal. And I looked at what my heart was telling me.

He said he believed me, but I didn't believe him. He had always lied and said things based on his own needs and wants. Now here he was, a lonesome person at the end of his life. No one else would visit him. It was easier for him to say that he believed me than it would have been for him to be alone. I was left with the decision of what—if any—kind of relationship I wanted to have with him.

That's when I realized that I had been at battle with my father my whole life. But my fear of him was the fear I had felt at seven or eleven confronted by a vital, middle-aged man. Now he was an old, toothless man, dependent on me. I could get off the battlefield if I chose to.

choices

A little while later, the people at the home called. My dad was failing, his memory was going, and he needed more care. They were kicking him out. I could have put him in any number of impersonal places or let the social workers at the Veterans Administration handle his care. But I wanted to be bigger than that. I'd been given so much love in my life, I felt I had a certain standard to live up to. And I understood that as long as I held on to my anger at him, the battle would never really be over.

What happened in my childhood, that wasn't about power or love. My father was diseased and weak. What he did was wrong. But now I was the one in charge. I could step in and do things differently.

I would not fault anyone for making a different choice, but I decided to look after my father. I found him a very good place to live. I started visiting him. I brought him clothes and things he needed. It wasn't a warm and fuzzy "He's my daddy" kind of thing, but I gave him the dignity I'd want any older person to have at the end of life.

And now that he's gone, I know I did the right thing for me, too. There's no unfinished business between us. It feels done.

When I think back, I wonder if he wasn't telling the truth, in a way, when he said he didn't remember. I wonder if, along with those beatings in his childhood, he might have been sexually assaulted as well. If I dissociated so profoundly, he might have done so, too. It was hard enough for me to remember what happened and piece it all together. And I had the advantages of education and therapy and emotional support. For a man in his time in history and with his limited resources, it could have been impossible.

I do believe the world is set up so that we have free will. We're learning the consequences of making certain kinds of choices. I didn't have a choice about being abused. It happened and I coped the best way I could at the time. Free will comes in the place where I get to say "I've been abused. Now what are my choices? I can either pass it along or I can heal from it and stop it."

Looking back through the generations of my family, I can see a very clear chain of events that go from my body back to slavery. The violence my father visited upon me was in some form the violence his father visited upon him, which was the violence he and his forebears experienced—the beatings, the dehumanizing, the ownership.

My father chose not to beat his children; that was a big link in the chain that he broke. And the sexual abuse, that ends with me.

Aaron, Emily, and Jeanne

Aaron: For me, it isn't enough to do my own healing. We live in a world where sexual abuse is happening to kids every day and I want to change that.

Here at college, working with SAFE, I can do something concrete about it. When I set up the Clothesline Project or give a workshop, I'm helping to make people more aware, to make this campus more friendly to survivors, to make this something we can all talk about.

And my activism has become an important part of my own healing. When I do this work, I take something that hurt me and isolated me in high school and transform it. I take that anger and I turn it around, turn it into action, use it as a catalyst to try and change the world.

safe at smith

Emily: So, to start with the basics, SAFE stands for Survivors and Allies for Education on Childhood Sexual Abuse and Incest. We're a student organization on the Smith College campus.

Jeanne: The three of us joined last year during our first semester here.

Aaron: We're trying to deal with the fact that sexual abuse and incest are so hushed up, such taboo topics.

On our campus—on any high school or college campus—there are so many survivors and so many other people who have been affected, directly or indirectly. They don't talk about it. They keep it inside.

But an important part of healing is getting the subject out in the open. That's true whether you're talking about one person trying to heal, or a community, or a whole society. It's impossible to heal if you don't have basic information. You need an atmosphere where it's okay to talk about these things.

I was still in high school when I first got involved with SAFE. It was the weekend when high school seniors come to check out the campus. SAFE was having their Spring Awareness Week at the same time and I was staying with a friend from home who was a member. She said, "We're going to get up at five in the morning and hang up T-shirts for the Clothesline Project."

I thought she was crazy. It was cold and semidark when we got out there. We pinned up all these shirts, hundreds of them. I ended up staying and helping out at the information table all day.

Coming from high school, this was just what I wanted, a campus where people were trying to change things. And it was reassuring to know that I wouldn't be the only person who wanted to deal with survivor issues.

is this abuse?

Aaron: I like it that SAFE is survivors and allies working together. I don't have to tell my story to do this work. I can just go out and put on events, show movies, lead discussions. What I have to say isn't lim-

ited by my experiences. But it doesn't have to be totally impersonal either. I can choose how much I disclose and when.

I was fifteen when I was raped. He was a friend, not some grownup taking advantage of me. And it wasn't my first sexual experience either. So I didn't consider it child sexual abuse at the time. I spent a lot of energy when I was fifteen trying to convince myself that it was no big deal.

But it was.

It changed me. I needed to give myself the time and attention to heal.

Sometimes it's so hard to see that in yourself! The clincher for me was when I asked myself, "If my best friend came to me and described this scenario, would I recognize it as abuse? Yes. Would I try to help?

Yes. Then maybe I should do that for myself as well." So I did get help, from my family and a counselor.

Now I speak out as a survivor. It isn't always easy being publicly identified with this issue. It's like being out about other parts of your personal life. You need friends, a community around you that supports and accepts you as you are. Other people may have all kinds of misunderstandings about what it means to be an abuse survivor. You have to recognize that their opinions and biases are their problems, not yours, and not let them stand in your way.

I think a really big part of healing is to acknowledge the power that a traumatic event like rape or abuse can have over you, and give voice to yourself, and then take that and go with it wherever you choose. Do something positive.

harassment

Jeanne: I don't feel that I have to identify as a survivor or as not-a-survivor when I do this work, but personal experience is definitely part of what brought me here.

Rape, incest, and child sexual abuse are at one end of a continuum of ways that people treat each other badly. Like a lot of people, I've had other kinds of sexual experiences that left me feeling bad about myself. There were times when I didn't know I could say no.

I definitely experienced a lot of sexual harassment starting in fifth grade, and on through sixth, seventh, and eighth grade. I was the girl in my class who developed first; by fifth grade I was five feet two inches and had breasts. It was not fun. Boys didn't know how to react to somebody who looked physically more mature. I got lots of verbal slurs, like "She's a slut," and a lot of physical groping, things like just walking down the hall and somebody touches your breast.

Now I think about that and I wonder, "How can people think that's okay?" But then I didn't really know it wasn't okay either. I felt very uncomfortable and upset, but I didn't think there were ways to stop it. And I didn't know other, better ways to be recognized as a sexual person.

Activism began for me as a coping mechanism. I started doing feminist organizing when I was fifteen. I was doing activism around welfare and other things that weren't even a part of my personal life. I was advocating for other people because I didn't know how to advocate for myself.

Now I work on women's health issues. Last year I was involved with peer sex education; that's where you learn about healthy sex, safe sex, and good communication and then teach it to your peers. After I got involved in SAFE, I helped incorporate survivor issues into the peer-sex-ed workshops because they hadn't really addressed childhood sexual abuse before.

an ally

Emily: Joining SAFE was different for me. I wasn't an activist and I didn't have experience with the subject of abuse. But right before I left home for college, one of my friends confided in me that she was sexually abused. When she told me, I didn't know what to say to her. I didn't know what to do about it. I felt so helpless. When I left for school I was really torn up.

Then, near the first week of college, when you really don't know anyone but you know you should get involved, there was this activities fair on campus. The SAFE material looked interesting. I wanted to know more.

But going to the first meeting was scary. There were maybe twenty-five people in the room. The older students were so knowledgeable. I thought, "I don't know anything about this. I'm not a survivor. I haven't done anything like this before."

I wasn't really sure if I was supposed to be there. I mean, they said "survivors and allies," but was that true? Or was I the only person in the room who *hadn't* been abused?

The only reason I came back was because of my friend. I stayed and helped out a little and then got more involved. Now I'm cohead with Aaron! How crazy is that? When I went to that first meeting I never would have predicted that I'd be heading the organization within two years.

Aaron: When people come to their first SAFE meeting, we try to make it clear that we are not a support group for survivors. This isn't group therapy. We're not trained as counselors or crisis workers.

Emily: But we are supportive. At every meeting we have a check-in where people say something about what's going on in their daily lives, so we get to know each other. If people haven't eaten, we send out for Chinese food or a pizza. We're aware that everyone is already overcommitted and—on top of everything else—we're working on a stressful issue.

Aaron: There's a core group of people who take on loads of responsibility for things like organizing workshops and writing flyers. Other people help out and some just listen. Then, when we need someone to put up posters or stuff envelopes, someone who has been sitting there quietly for months will say "I can do that." We need everyone.

Jeanne: Outside of the meetings, we might talk about personal experiences, but the meetings are for planning. What events do we have coming up? Are any workshops scheduled? Who is going to present them?

Emily: We give the workshops throughout the year at the different residential houses on campus. Three of us put it on together.

The first thing we do is pass around our handouts so that everyone has basic information. One sheet is "How to Help Yourself" and on the back is "How to Help a Friend." There's a sheet with emergency phone numbers on and off campus and a list of therapists in the area.

We define terms like *incest* and *molestation* and give statistics on the prevalence of child sexual abuse.

Aaron: When people hear the statistics—one in three girls and one in six boys—their faces register shock. They think about how many kids they've babysat and their siblings and their cousins and their peers and they realize how many people they must know who have been through something like this.

The workshop is interactive. Instead of telling people about coping mechanisms, we'll ask, "What ways do you think children might cope with abuse?" People call out things like "Pretend it didn't happen," "Blame themselves," "Get help," and we write them on a big piece of butcher paper and ask, "What do you think the effects of this might be?" and "How about in terms of self-image? Relationships?" People open up and start talking.

Emily: The hottest topic is recovered memories. We talk about why children might forget and how it can help them—at least for a while. We discuss the studies that show how abuse gets repressed, and how often that happens, and how memory comes back sometimes in fragments.

Aaron: The workshop lasts an hour or so and it's packed with information and discussion. There's a sense of accomplishment when you finish, because you feel like you've opened people's eyes.

Emily: And knowledge is contagious. If people feel they can talk about it here, that means they can go back to wherever they're from and talk about it with their friends from high school, their siblings, their parents. They can break the taboo.

Sometimes people will disclose abuse to us. We're not crisis workers, but we can give the kind of support that an informed friend would give. We listen. I think that's the most important thing, just to listen and believe and offer support.

Sometimes people feel "crazy" because what happened to them is so outside the norm of what people around them expect. We let them know that they are responding normally to a crazy situation. We tell them that the abuse is not their fault. And we respect boundaries. Some people who have been abused do not want to be touched. You have to ask first.

One thing that we feel is really important is to respect each person's confidentiality. Not just their identity, but their story; and to not re-peat it, because they own it.

And we direct them to local counselors who deal specifically with child abuse. There are national organizations and help lines they can call, too. It's really important for people to know that they are not alone and that there is a lot of help available.

Emily: Throughout the year we put on events, but twice a year we have Sexual Abuse Awareness Week, when we do a whole variety of things.

Aaron: We show movies like *Eve's Bayou*, *Bastard out of Carolina*, *The Color Purple*, *Antonia's Line*, and have discussions afterward. We make and sell T-shirts and pass out buttons.

Jeanne: We've had poetry readings, dance workshops, guest speakers from off campus, and roundtable discussions. We try to tie our events in to what people are studying, like a creative writing class might come to hear an author speak.

During Spring Awareness Week we put up our Clothesline Project. The snow is melting, some years it's even warm, and there are all these colorful T-shirts flying like flags in the air.

Emily: Our Clothesline Project is part of a national project where people make T-shirts that testify to their experience of abuse and as-sault. Nationally it is about violence against women and children. Here, we focus on childhood sexual abuse and rape.

Aaron: It's a way of airing society's dirty laundry.

Emily: And it stops people from just being unaware. It says, "This is important. It's a part of a lot of people's lives right here."

hundreds of shirts

Aaron: Our clothesline is set up around the perimeter of one of the big lawns on campus. We get up at five o'clock in the morning and, using clothespins, we pin up hundreds and hundreds of T-shirts made by present and past students, professors, and staff.

Our table is at the edge of the lawn. We take turns sitting there and talking with people, giving them handouts and advertising the other events we are doing that week. Inside the enclosed space, there's another table where people can make their own shirt to add to the project. We supply T-shirts and fabric markers, paint, and puffy paint.

Some people come in with a little crumpled-up piece of paper and on it they have their vision of what their shirt is going to look like, or they have a poem or a letter they've written. Sometimes people address their offender, writing things they never got to say because they were too young or they didn't know how or they tried and no one listened. I've seen people bring in shirts they've spent hours on at home. Others just pick up a shirt and freestyle.

Emily: Some of the shirts are expressions of rage; one is a giant "NO!" Another says, "You may have ruined my night, but I *won't* let you ruin my life!" There are shirts with messages about pride and love and strength, so you know that some people are really thriving.

Jeanne: I think it's really important that we only have shirts from our school because usually survivors are so invisible. This way, it really hits you. All these shirts—and there are hundreds and hundreds of them— these are all experiences of people I sit with in class and I eat next to in the dining hall or who went to school here before me. You have a sense of connection with all these other people.

Aaron: We set out this bound note-book each year, so people can write down their responses. One person wrote—in effect—"Screw you SAFE for doing this right before finals when I need to concentrate on studying!" Many more write things like "Thanks, this means a lot to me" and "I'm a survivor, too. It's really hard to look at the shirts, but I make myself do it every year to remind myself of how far I've come."

Some people sign their name or draw a picture. Sometimes they write about their own experience with abuse. They might not want to make a T-shirt or tell their story to someone face-to-face, but seeing the project brings up feelings and they want to tell someone, so they write it in the book.

Emily: Activism isn't for everyone. I like working one-on-one best, so this may be the only activism I ever do, but I'm glad I'm doing it.

Being in SAFE has certainly changed me. When I came to school here, I was really shy. But talking about a difficult subject has made it a lot easier for me to speak up. I mean, if you can be comfortable talking about sexual abuse, you can talk about anything!

It's definitely increased my empathy, too. I realize there can be a lot more to a person than what you see on the surface. People are dealing

with all kinds of difficult things in their lives, things you might never know about.

Child sexual abuse is such a big problem and it's so pervasive. There are times when you feel like you haven't really changed things at all, at least not on the bigger scale.

But we can't expect little children to stop abuse. And offenders don't just magically disappear. It takes a whole lot of people working on this in a lot of different ways to make the world safer for kids. Attitudes have to change. The first step for that is education. That's what we're doing, the first step.

Jeanne: When SAFE started up here, it was seen as threatening. The Clothesline Project was especially controversial because it's so out

there. You can't miss it. And reading the shirts can be a very emotional experience. But as our collection of T-shirts grew, people could see that this really is something we need to talk about in a whole lot of ways. Now there are so many people—faculty and staff as well as students—who tell us how glad they are that we're here.

Aaron: Our college president came by the clothesline twice this year to cheer us on. And it was amazing to hear the campus day-care teacher explain the T-shirts to a group of little kids. She said that the shirts were made by people who'd been hurt and this was their way of telling their stories and saying that what happened to them was not okay and that making the shirts helped them feel better. She used the occasion to talk with the kids about safe touch, too.

For me, this work feels good, but it's also hard. There's stress in being an activist, regardless of the issue you are working on. The whole point of social justice activism is that there's something really messed up and we want to change it. That means dealing with things that most people want to ignore, coming up against people's resistance to change.

My mom says that everything I do is too serious! And sometimes I do get bummed out. I look around and think, "God, this world is so messed up!" But activism is one way to make things better.

I love being a rockin' activist, somebody who is passionate and motivated and out there doing this work. I get to feel a little piece of the power of change. I get to say, "There is something going on in my generation and it's good. We can do this." It gives me hope.

Help!

IF YOU'VE BEEN ABUSED, if you are concerned about your own or someone else's safety, or if you need to sort through your feelings, you can call these hotlines at any time of the day or night. All calls are anonymous and confidential.

Childhelp USA
800-4-A-CHILD *or* 800-422-4453

Choose option 1 to speak to a professional counselor who will listen to you and help you figure out what to do.

National Sexual Assault Hotline
800-656-HOPE *or* 800-656-4673

This number will connect you to a crisis center near you.

Suicide Hotline
800-SUICIDE *or* 800-784-2433

At any time of the night or day you can talk with someone who understands suicidal feelings and can help you survive.

Kids Help Phone (in Canada)
800-668-6868 or call your local crisis center.

Where to Go for More

THESE BOOKS, MOVIES, ORGANIZATIONS, AND WEB SITES explore aspects of abuse and healing that appear in the interviews in this book. For more information about *Strong at the Heart* and for additional resources, visit www.StrongAtTheHeart.com.

Stories of Healing and Hope

True Stories

Finding Fish: A Memoir, by Antwone Fisher (New York: William Morrow, 2001).
   Born to a mother in prison, Antwone Fisher was abandoned by her to foster care, where he was emotionally and sexually abused. At eighteen he was on the street and in search of a way to save himself.

A Girl's Life Online, by Katherine Tarbox (New York: Plume, 2004). The eighteen-year-old author writes about being seduced online when she was thirteen into a relationship with a middle-aged pedophile who posed as a much younger "friend."

I Know Why the Caged Bird Sings, by Maya Angelou (New York: Random House, 1970; reissued by Bantam in 1993).
   This vivid and unflinching memoir of the poet's childhood centers on a violent rape when she was eight, her silent healing

in her grandmother's care, and her passionate connection with words.

Incidents in the Life of a Slave Girl, by Harriet Jacobs (New York, London: Signet Classic, 2000; first published in 1861).
Harriet was born a slave; her master, Dr. Flint, had complete control over every aspect of her life. To escape his sexual abuses, Harriet used all of the resources she could muster. This first-person account tells what slavery was really like for African-Americans and how one fiercely determined girl escaped.

Learning to Swim, by Ann Turner (New York: Scholastic, 2000).
"With these poems, I have taken a painful, silent time in my childhood and transformed it into something healing and life-giving," says the author of this verse narrative.

Ophelia Speaks: Adolescent Girls Write about Their Search for Self, by Sara Shandler (New York: HarperCollins, 1999).
Girls twelve to eighteen write about their lives, including how they feel about their bodies, their families, their friends, and the challenges—including sexual abuse—that many face. The author was sixteen when she started this project.

Where I Stopped: Remembering an Adolescent Rape, by Martha Ramsey (New York: Harcourt Brace, 1995).
Poet Martha Ramsey looks back on the summer she was thirteen, when she was raped by a neighbor. A delicate exploration of her own emotions, her family's response, and her struggle to come to terms with her offender.

Fiction

The Color Purple, by Alice Walker (New York: Harcourt Brace Jovanovich, 1982).

Abused and raped as a child, separated from the sister she loves, Celie struggles to survive until her friendship with Shug inspires her to create a new and satisfying life for herself. This deeply moving novel of self-discovery received both the Pulitzer Prize and the National Book Award.

Forged by Fire, by Sharon Draper (New York: Simon and Schuster, 1997).

Gerald tries to save his little sister from their abusive stepfather in this second book in the Hazelwood High trilogy.

I Hadn't Meant to Tell You This and ***Lena***, by Jacqueline Woodson (New York: Delacorte, 1994 and 1999).

In the first book, Lena tells her only friend, Marie, that her father is sexually abusing her. Marie, shocked, responds with questions and compassion, but she cannot rescue her friend. Lena does the only thing she can to save herself and her little sister. The second book describes their desperate flight and the help that the two white girls find in the African-American community.

I Was a Teenage Fairy, by Francesca Lia Block (New York: HarperCollins, 1998).

In the glitzy, glamorous world of Hollywood, child actors and models are fair game for all kinds of exploitation. Barbie (named for the doll) learns to fight back. Wise, funny, and magical.

Life Is Funny, by E. R. Frank (New York: DK Ink, 2000).

Interconnected stories of eleven diverse teens unfold over the course of seven years in this moving and quirky novel. Each chapter is a stand-alone story of a young person facing tough situations and making hard choices.

The Lovely Bones, by Alice Sebold (New York: Little, Brown, 2002).

Fourteen-year-old Susie Salmon, the narrator of this novel, is already dead. From heaven, she observes her family and friends as they struggle in the aftermath of her rape and murder. The violence and grief in this adult novel are heartbreaking, but there is also sweetness as—even in heaven—people work through their losses and move on.

Push, by Sapphire (New York: Knopf, 1996).

Precious Jones is an illiterate sixteen-year-old, pregnant for the second time by her own father. As she learns to read and write, she begins to take control of her life. Strong language. Brutally honest.

Silver, by Norma Fox Mazer (New York: William Morrow, 1988).

Over the course of one challenging year, Sarabeth Silver forms friendships with a group of girls at a posh junior high school. When one of the girls reveals she's being abused by her socially prominent uncle, Silver and her friends try to help.

Telling, by Marilyn Reynolds (Buena Park, CA: Morning Glory Press, 1996).

After the father of the kids she babysits for first kisses and then starts touching her sexually, twelve-year-old Cassie confides in her older cousin Lisa. This book gives an honest picture of the aftermath of disclosure—how people's lives get more complicated at first, but ultimately better.

Treacherous Love, by Beatrice Sparks, Ph.D. (New York: Avon Books, 2000).

Fourteen-year-old Jennie is having a rough time until she meets a wonderful teacher, Mr. Johnstone, who takes an increasingly personal interest in her.

Whale Talk, by Chris Crutcher (New York: HarperCollins, 2001).

Tri-racial high school senior T. J. Jones builds a swim team of misfits at a school with no swimming pool, confronts small-town racism, and fights to save an abused child—and does it all with dark humor and keen intelligence.

When Jeff Comes Home, by Catherine Atkins (New York: Putnam, 1999).

Two and a half years after he was kidnapped by a pedophile, sixteen-year-old Jeff comes home. How can he ever fit into his family again? How can he ever tell anyone what happened to him while he was gone?

When She Hollers, by Cynthia Voigt (New York: Scholastic, 1996).

Tish, a high school senior, struggles to survive the emotional effects of sexual abuse by her stepfather. Over the course of a single day she figures out the one true thing that will save her sanity and her life. Intense.

Film

Antwone Fisher, directed by and starring Denzel Washington (Twentieth Century Fox, 2002); rated PG-13.

The true story of Antwone Fisher's triumph over childhood abandonment and abuse is somewhat fictionalized. The movie focuses on the young adult Antwone's relationship with a navy psychiatrist who pushes the young seaman to confront his past so that he can connect with the girl he loves.

The Color Purple, directed by Steven Spielberg, starring Whoopi Goldberg, Danny Glover, and Oprah Winfrey (MGM, 1985); rated PG-13.

Based on the award-winning novel by Alice Walker.

Forever Fourteen, written and directed by Kelly St. John (Santa Monica, CA: Pyramid Media, 2001); *www.pyramidmedia.com*; winner of the 23rd Annual News & Documentary Emmy Award for Outstanding Informational Programming.

Kelly St. John explores the impact of the abduction and rape she experienced on her own family and on the family of murder victim Wendy Osborn. This is the film Kelly talks about in her chapter.

Hollow Water, directed by Bonnie Dickie, produced by Joe Mac-Donald (Montreal: National Film Board of Canada, 2000); *www.nfb.ca.*

In a tiny Native village in northern Canada, parents and teens talk about their experiences in healing circles based on traditional Ojib-way culture. This film is a testimony to one community's determination to reach out to offenders and victims and to heal the whole village. In her chapter Sheena describes these healing circles.

Monsoon Wedding, directed by Mira Nair (USA Films, 2002); rated R for language.

Three interlocking stories unfold as a family in India prepares for and celebrates a joyous traditional wedding. When Ria sees the uncle who molested her take an interest in a younger cousin, she and the family patriarch face difficult but ultimately satisfying decisions.

Rabbit-Proof Fence, directed by Phillip Noyce (Miramax, 2002); rated PG.

Based on the true story of three aboriginal girls in Australia who were forcibly removed from their families and their traditional way of life to be trained as servants. One scene indicates the sexual exploitation they face. Twelve-year-old Molly escapes with her sister and cousin and begins a heroic journey across Australia on foot.

Information about Abuse and Healing

Self-Help Books

Beginning to Heal: A First Book for Men and Women Who Were Sexually Abused as Children, by Laura Davis and Ellen Bass (New York: HarperCollins, 2003; revised edition).
Clear and concise, this book is an excellent road map to the healing process. It contains sound advice for survivors, friends, and family members. By the authors of the comprehensive guide to healing, *The Courage to Heal*.

How Long Does It Hurt? A Guide to Recovering from Incest and Sexual Abuse for Teenagers, Their Friends, and Their Families, by Cynthia Mather (San Francisco: Jossey-Bass, 1994).
Is this really abuse? What is it like to tell? What if you have to go to court? How do you move forward? Helpful advice for teens in all stages of dealing with sexual abuse.

No Secrets, No Lies: How Black Families Can Heal from Sexual Abuse, by Robin D. Stone (New York: Broadway Books, 2004).
This wise and powerful guide contains solid information on child sexual abuse. The personal stories, social insight, and practical help it contains are based in African-American experience.

When Something Feels Wrong: A Survival Guide about Abuse for Young People, by Deanna S. Pledge, Ph.D. (Minneapolis: Free Spirit, 2003).

Covers a wide range of abuses—physical, sexual, and emotional abuse, date rape, bullying, and neglect. Detailed advice about who and how to tell, what happens after you tell, and how to start healing.

Help Organizations

Childhelp USA
hotline: 800-4-A-CHILD *or* 800-422-4453
office line: 480-922-8212
15757 N. 78th Street, Scottsdale, AZ 85260
www.childhelpusa.org

You can call the hotline night or day to talk with a professional counselor for free. The Web site answers questions about the hotline, tells how it works in both English and Spanish, and describes other Childhelp programs.

Kids Help Phone
kids' help line: 800-668-6868
parents' help line: 888-603-9100
for calls from outside Canada: 416-586-0100
www.kidshelp.sympatico.ca

Canada's toll-free, 24-hour, bilingual (English/French) phone counseling service for children and youth. Professional counselors provide immediate support to young people in urban and rural communities across the country. You can also go to their Web site and post messages or receive online counseling. All services are confidential and free.

RAINN (Rape, Abuse and Incest National Network)
hotline: 800-656-HOPE *or* 800-656-4673
www.rainn.org

RAINN Operates the National Sexual Assault Hotline. The Web site includes statistics, counseling resources, prevention tips, and a page of advice for rape victims and their friends.

SNAP (Survivors Network of those Abused by Priests)

877-SNAP HEALS *or* 877-762-7432

P.O. Box 6416, Chicago, IL 60680-6416

www.snapnetwork.org

This is the organization that Jonathan joins in chapter 2. SNAP provides support for survivors of abuse by clergy, educates the public, and works for reforms within the church and society.

Understanding Abuse and Its Effects

David Baldwin's Trauma Information Pages

www.trauma-pages.com

Hundreds of articles and links on this site cover aspects of trauma from sexual abuse to war and terrorism. Information on post-traumatic stress, dissociation, and what happens to people's brains when they experience trauma.

Everything You Need to Know about Dealing with Sexual Assault,

by Laura Kaminker (New York: Rosen, 2000; revised edition).

This easy-to-read book for teens dispels myths about rape and abuse and gives advice about staying safe.

Jim Hopper's Home Page

www.jimhopper.com

Dr. Jim Hopper is a research fellow at Harvard Medical School. His pages include statistics on childhood sexual abuse, information for male survivors, and a very thorough review of scientific research on recovered memory for child abuse. Good links.

National Clearinghouse on Child Abuse and Neglect Information
330 C Street SW, Washington, DC 20447
800-FYI-3366 *or* 703-385-7565
nccanch.acf.hhs.gov
> Fact sheets, resource lists, and publications on abuse and child maltreatment can be downloaded here. Some materials are in Spanish.

The Recovered Memory Project
www.recoveredmemory.org
> Dr. Ross E. Cheit, a professor at Brown University, established this scholarly site to document cases of recovered memory and discuss the controversy over the repression of memory of abuse.

Trauma and Recovery, by Judith Herman, M.D. (New York: Harper-Collins, 1992).
> How does human-induced trauma affect people? How do people heal? This scholarly book by a Harvard professor of psychiatry brings together research on survivors of wars, concentration camps, and abuse in the home to give a full picture of healing in the aftermath of violence.

Date and Acquaintance Rape

Coping with Date and Acquaintance Rape, by Andrea Parrot (New York: Rosen, 1999; revised edition).
> Despite the lurid cover on the new edition, this book is full of helpful information for teens.

I Never Called It Rape: The Ms. Report on Recognizing, Fighting, and Surviving Date and Acquaintance Rape, by Robin

Warshaw (New York: Harper and Row, 1988; HarperPerennial edition, 1994).

Based on the groundbreaking Ms. Magazine Campus Project on Sexual Assault, this book examines social attitudes that foster sexual violence against teens and young women. Eye-opening statistics and moving personal stories.

In Love and Danger: A Teen's Guide to Breaking Free of Abusive Relationships, by Barrie Levy (Seattle: Seal Press, 1993 and 1997). Does your boyfriend or girlfriend hurt you? Have you hurt someone you love? Good advice on how to break the cycle of violence.

For Boys and Men

When Teenage Boys Have Been Sexually Abused: A Guide for Teenagers (Vancouver: Family Services of Greater Vancouver, 1991). Available from the National Clearinghouse on Family Violence, Health Canada.

from Canada: 800-267-1291

from the United States: 613-957-2938

Or download as a PDF file at: *www.hc-sc.gc.ca/hppb/familyviolence/nfntsabus_e.html*

One of a series of informational booklets on sexual abuse, this publication addresses teenage boys' concerns. Direct and honest.

MaleSurvivor

www.malesurvivor.org

Dedicated to overcoming the sexual victimization of men and boys, this organization gives conferences and retreats and puts out a newsletter that you can access at its Web site.

Victims No Longer: Men Recovering from Incest and Other Sexual Child Abuse, by Mike Lew (New York: HarperCollins, 2004, 2nd edition).

In this excellent resource Lew answers questions like: What is abuse? Can boys be abused by women? What is the relationship between sexuality, homophobia, and shame? Is recovery possible? (The answer to the last question is *yes*—and he tells how.)

Youthful Offenders

Adolescent Sex Offenders—Overview Paper, by Frederick Mathews (Ottawa: National Clearinghouse on Family Violence, Health Canada, 1997). Download this and other excellent publications at *www.hc-sc.gc.ca/hppb/familyviolence/nfntsabus_e.html*

Who are adolescent sex offenders? Why do they offend? How can they stop? This article gives the basics and refers you to further reading.

Sasian

www.sasian.org

e-mail: info@sasian.org

Sasian raises awareness of physical, sexual, and emotional abuse by brothers and sisters. Site includes material on sibling sexual abuse in four languages. Extensive links.

Stop It Now!

888-PREVENT *or* 888-773-8368

www.stopitnow.com

This organization addresses child sexual abuse at the source—offenders, including youthful offenders. "We do not see child sex abusers as monsters, but as (people) who are responsible for their criminal behavior and who can choose to stop the abuse." The help line is staffed during business hours. All calls are confidential.

We Are Not Monsters: Teens Speak Out about Teens in Trouble, by Sabrina Solin Weill (New York: HarperTempest, 2002).

An unblinking look at kids dealing with really tough stuff, including murder, suicide, teen-adult sexual relations, self-injury, and sexual offending.

Resources for Making Choices, Building Strength, and Changing the World

Sexuality

Advocates for Youth

www.advocatesforyouth.org

This Web site is dedicated to helping young people make informed and responsible decisions about their reproductive and sexual health. Written in part by teens. In English, Spanish, and French.

Changing Bodies, Changing Lives: A Book for Teens on Sex and Relationships, by Ruth Bell et al. (New York: Random House, 1998; 3rd edition).

A thorough guide for both boys and girls.

Free Your Mind: The Book for Gay, Lesbian, and Bisexual Youth —and Their Allies, by Ellen Bass and Kate Kaufman (New York: HarperPerennial; 1996).

Sound advice for gay and questioning teens.

Sex, Etc.

www.sexetc.org

This Web site is written for teens by teens and is sponsored by the Network for Family Life Education at Rutgers University. Solid information about all aspects of sexuality, including abuse, homosexuality, and sexual response. Downloadable newsletter.

Drugs and Alcohol

Alanon/Alateen
toll-free meeting information line: 888-425-2666
www.al-anon.alateen.org
> For family and friends of alcoholics. Peer support meetings for teens who are dealing with the alcoholism of family members or friends. Web site in English, Spanish, and French. Pages for teens.

Go Ask Alice
www.goaskalice.columbia.edu
> At this Columbia University Web site you can find answers to all kinds of health questions, including how to deal with drugs and alcohol.

Nar-Anon, Nar-Anon Family Group Headquarters, Inc.
toll-free: 800-477-6291; *or* 310-547-5800
22527 Crenshaw Blvd. #200B, Torrance, CA 90505
www.nar-anon.org
> Support groups for families and friends of people with drug problems. Some states have groups especially for teens.

Narcotics Anonymous, World Service
818-773-9999
P.O. Box 9999, Van Nuys, CA 91409
www.na.org

A 12-step self-help recovery program for people of all ages who are involved with drugs.

Resilience

33 Things Every Girl Should Know: Stories, Songs, Poems and Smart Talk by 33 Extraordinary Women, edited by Tonya Bolden (New York: Crown, 1998).

Cartoonists, entertainers, and authors, including Lynda Barry, Sharon Creech, M. E. Kerr, and Sandra Cisneros, write stories—and draw pictures—that inform girls and inspire inner strength.

On Playing a Poor Hand Well: Insights from the Lives of Those Who Have Overcome Childhood Risks and Adversities, by Mark Katz (New York, London: Norton, 1997).

A lot of people have rotten childhoods. Some turn their lives around, others don't. The author uses both personal stories and research on resiliency to show how people succeed in taking control of their lives.

Project Resilience

www.projectresilience.com

"We promote a strengths-based approach to both youth and adults struggling to overcome hardship . . . family disruption, poverty, violence, substance abuse, and racism." Although this site is designed for educators, the "Core Concepts" can help anyone looking for ways to build a better life for themselves.

Resiliency for Teens

helping.apa.org

American Psychological Association Web page. Ten good ideas for increasing your ability to make it through hard times and take charge of your life.

Teens Write Through It: Essays from Teens Who Have Triumphed over Trouble (Minneapolis: Fairview Press, 1998).

Fifty-eight short, personal stories by teens cover all kinds of challenges, from coping with racism and family problems to achieving self-esteem.

Activism

The Clothesline Project

P.O. Box 654, Brewster, MA 02631

www.clotheslineproject.org

This national organization has helped more than five hundred local groups start their own Clothesline projects, including SAFE at Smith. This site also includes information on teen dating, supporting survivors, and the Dating Bill of Rights.

Generation Five

www.generationfive.org

A youth-friendly organization that trains activists and grassroots organizers to help end child sexual abuse in their own communities.

It's Our World, Too! Young People Who Are Making a Difference; How They Do It—How You Can, Too!, by Phillip Hoose (New York: Farrar, Straus and Giroux, 2002; paperback edition).

Profiles of teens and children who have successfully campaigned for social and political change.

SAFE at Smith

http://sophia.smith.edu/safe

The student organization described by Aaron, Emily, and Jean runs this Web site. It includes information from their flyers and links to rape crisis centers nationwide.

Take Back the News
www.TakeBackTheNews.net

This young activist Web site encourages survivors to raise public awareness of rape and sexual abuse.

TeenPCAR
Pennsylvania Coalition Against Rape
TeenPCAR.com

This Web site offers a subscription to *Teen Esteem* magazine, a CD of music by young artists who address sexual violence, and ideas for how you can help stop sexual violence and harassment at your school.

Youth! The 26% Solution, by Wendy Schaetzel Lesko and Emanuel Tsouriunis II (Kensington, MD: Youth Activism 2000 Project, 1998).

800-543-7693

www.youthactivism.com

To carry out effective activism, you need to know how to strategize, plan events, get publicity, and deal with adults who may not want to listen—yet. This book tells how.

Acknowledgments

THE ELEVEN PEOPLE YOU HAVE JUST MET TRUSTED ME with their personal experiences in the hope of helping others. This book belongs to them.

Many people contributed to this project. Other survivors shared their histories with me and—although they could not all be included—their insights helped shape the final book. Professionals, teens, parents, and writing friends read drafts, answered questions, advised, and encouraged me. I am especially indebted to Carmela Wenger, M.F.T.; Eugene Porter, author of *Treating Sexually Abused Boys*; Connie Valentine, president of the California Protective Parents Association; Antoinette Martin, M.A., school psychologist; Sarah Page; Morgan Lynn; Robert Stevens; Charlene Hanson, pastor of the Coastline Foursquare Church; Kathy Dreyer; Lori Keele; Marie Raphael; Heather, Aurora, Anna, Oshen, Warren, and Kim; Shellye, Margie, and Heidi; Noel and Annemarie Munn; Caroline and Jessie; Dr. Tom Meyer; Xandie and Fiona Zublin-Meyer; Marilyn Murphy; Jan Hodgman; Ellen Land-Weber and Cecelia Holland.

For connecting me with survivors who appear in this book I am grateful to Jeannette Cook, Community Holistic Circle Healing; David Clohessy and Buddy Cotton, Survivors Network of those Abused by Priests; Patrick Sweeney, Launchpad; Staci Haines, Generation Five; and Stephen Braveman, M.F.T.

Merle Davis and Sarah Page transcribed interviews with care. Paul Swenson and Matt Salcido provided technical assistance on the photography. Miss Blizzard and Jacob and Benjamin Lehman were my home-based editorial team.

Melanie Kroupa recognized the importance of sharing these stories and—along with the talented people at FSG—made this book come true.

On this project, as in all our endeavors, my husband, Peter Lehman, has been my confidant, coach, and best friend.